BERGDORF GOODMAN

§§

M.D. Poole

Cover art by JC Media

BERGDORF GOODMAN

Life is a party. Dress like it.
— **Audrey Hepburn**

I'll tell you the truth and it's up to you to live with it.
-- **William Goldman, *The Princess Bride***

I was dismayed when I found out 'Type A' refers to a risk for heart disease. I thought it was just a nickname my mom gave me!
— **Reese Witherspoon**

Her reply when asked who she wanted to be like: "I'd like other people to be like me."
— **11 year old Serena Williams**

BERGDORF GOODMAN

"He's awake," Chloé said. She took ahold of my hand.

"It's about time," Nana said without getting out of her chair. "What do you think you're doing, interrupting my work for the entire day?"

"Nana, stop. She's joking, Daddy," Chloé said. "They called us. Thank goodness you had us listed as emergency contacts."

The lights were bright white, and I had a white sheet up to my neck.

"I've told Cary a million times that I'd outlast you. You're too fat, Andy." That was Nana talking again.

"Nana," Chloé begged, "stop. She's worried, Daddy. You know, she gets mean when she's worried."

I looked at Chloé's face and tried to ask what was going on, but I was too tired. When I focused again, a tall man holding a tablet stood next to me.

"Ah, Mr. Brown. Your daughter told me you opened your eyes."

The man was wearing a mask and had light brown eyes. He looked at me as if I were supposed to say something.

Finally, the tall man filled in the silence, "I'm Bradley Matthews. Do you know where you are?"

I moved my eyes to the ceiling, then to the side.

"You're in Mount Sinai West Hospital. Do you remember coming here?"

The guy was a bore. I closed my eyes.

"You had a heart attack at work, Mr. Brown. Can you tell me where you work?"

Bergdorf Goodman. I paused and wondered if I had answered out loud. Maybe I was dreaming.

"Well, you relax. The doctor will be in to see you again this afternoon," the man said.

§§

I saw a woman in a white jacket. No, not a jacket. A long white bathrobe. I felt confused and closed my eyes.

"Mr. Brown," a loud female voice demanded, "Mr. Brown, look at me."

I obeyed. She was blond. And young. Maybe 30 years old. Without make-up.

"You were very lucky. You arrived here within minutes after your heart attack. We inserted a catheter in your groin and put in two stents. You don't need a bypass at this time. You'll stay here a few days as a precautionary measure, and we'll begin a regimen of medications." She turned to the wall behind her, and I saw my mother and daughter standing there. "Will he take prescriptions as told?" she asked.

"He never does anything as told," Nana answered.

Chloé shushed her. "He will do everything you say, Dr. Park," she said. "I promise."

The blond turned back to me. "I'll see you tomorrow, Mr. Brown."

I took a breath, coughed, and closed my eyes.

3

§§

Conversation buzzed in the room like a swarm of nervous bees. I almost smiled when I picked out Chloé's voice, and Cary's with his accent. I didn't hear Nana, but two or three other voices were in the mix .

"When can I go back to work?" I asked. My voice sounded to me like it was wrapped in a wool muffler.

The buzz stopped.

Then it started again louder. "Daddy, you talked!" "What did you say?" "What did he say?" "Did he open his eyes?" "Let me get in there."

The last voice spoke softly, but it rang out like a command. "Mr. Brown, how are you feeling?"

I squinted. A tall, masked man with light brown eyes and a ponytail leaned over me.

I'd had my own ponytail a few years after I started at Bergdorf's. Tanya was pregnant and getting all the attention. Too much attention, so I decided to make myself feel better by letting my hair grow. A year later, even with baby Chloé in our lives, I was the center of attention. I wasn't the only salesperson with a ponytail, but I was the best. From the day I took the job, I had the highest sales figures and biggest client list. I chopped off the ponytail when my hairline started to recede.

"Do you remember me? I'm Bradley Matthews."

4

Truthfully, I had no idea who he was, but I put on my gracious host smile. "When can I go back to work?" I repeated. My voice sounded like soupy gravel.

"You have two stents to open the blockages that caused your heart attack. You'll have a regimen of medication, physical and mental therapy, and an appointment with me each week for 6 months. You can go home tomorrow and go back to work Monday if you wish."

"Daddy, that's great news!" Chloé chirped from the side of the bed opposite from the ponytail man. Her short hair spiked out in all directions. She blinked. Her myopic eyes looked giant behind her red frames. "I was so worried," she said. "I haven't left the hospital since you came in, Daddy. Stacy is covering my clients at work. Cary took Nana to the cafeteria 30 minutes ago; she'll be mad you woke up when she wasn't here. George is uncomfortable around sick people, but he called twice to wish you well."

She sighed like she'd been holding her breath, then said, "I am *so* glad you're going to be okay." She looked up and asked the ponytail man, "He'll be okay, right, Mr. Matthews?"

Ponytail man was wearing a lavender tie with green stripes. It looked like silk, Gucci probably, or Hermes. "I'll be back this afternoon," he said without answering my daughter and walked out of the room.

Entering the room three seconds after Ponytail left, my mother announced in a loud voice, "That tall drink of water is your cardiac nurse practitioner. He's like a doctor, but not." She plopped down in a chair and laughed derisively, "He's thinks he can get you healthy. Ha!"

Cary came in two steps behind Nana. "I'm glad to see you awake, Andy," he said kindly. He was 70, and a sexy old man. I'd never understood how he hooked up with my mother almost forty years back.

"Who's going to drive me home tomorrow?" I asked.

§§

My apartment was just how I'd left it four mornings before.

"Let's cheer this place up some," Chloé said. She flicked on the overhead lights and opened the maroon velvet curtains in the living room. She'd had me as a father for 26 years; you'd think she'd know I hated overhead lights. I turned on three table lamps and turned off the overhead switch.

She gave me the sideways glance that meant, "You're not cooperating," and pointed me to sit on the couch. "I'll make lunch."

"Don't you have clients or something? Maybe George needs his clothes washed?"

From the kitchen, she called out, "George does his own laundry. Stacy Peterson is covering for me at work. You've got me all day."

That felt like a death sentence. I loved my daughter, but she was very up-beat. Depressingly up-beat.

All I wanted to do was read my mail with my curtains closed and put on some jazz. Maybe Ella Fitzgerald. "Cry Me a River" would be good. But nooooo, I had to eat lunch with Chloé.

"So, how's work going?" I asked to turn the conversation away from me.

"Good, good, Daddy. I have more clients than I
…." It was lucky that Chloé had nice teeth since she smiled
all the time. She talked for a while about prosthetics and a
new ceramic elbow one of her doctors was testing. I
listened and nodded. Her pecan and avocado pasta salad
was surprisingly good, but it needed ranch dressing and
parmesan cheese.

Then I heard her say something about her
apartment. George was going to paint her bathroom? Was
this the George I knew? The lazy dull boyfriend?

"What did you say about George?"

Chloé smiled. "He said he wanted the apartment
freshened up before he moved in. I can't afford to hire a
painter, so he volunteered. Nice, huh?"

"He's moving in," I repeated.

She nodded and took a sip of seltzer water. "We're
not rushing. Maybe at the end of the month. Or early next
month."

"But you've only been with him, what, a couple of
weeks? That's rushing things."

"It's been six months, Daddy," she chuckled as if I
were a demented child. "Think how much rent we'll save.
It'll be like getting a raise."

I groaned silently. "Have you told your mother?"

"I called her last week. She's still living with the
producer, Hal Johnson. She said she might come visit soon.
You know, in honor of me cohabitating." She grinned.

Johnson was my ex-wife's fifth L.A. movie producer in eleven years. Tanya never lived alone and her partners were always rich.

I pushed my plate away and gave a fake yawn. "I think I need to take a nap, sweetie."

She was up out of her chair in a flash. "I'll turn down the bed."

"No, no. It'll be best if I get used to doing things for myself. In fact, why don't you go do what you need to do."

She looked at me sideways, considering. "I'll come back and make dinner. But only if you promise to keep your cell phone next to you on the nightstand."

I waved at her as I headed to the bedroom.

§§

The doorman buzzed me to say that Nana and Cary were waiting downstairs.

I had told Nana I didn't need help getting to my first heart attack support meeting, but she insisted on being my chaperone. Apparently, I had telegraphed that I was going to skip the stupid group session.

They had a taxi waiting when I got to the sidewalk.

"I could have done this by myself, you know," I grumbled. Nana didn't bother to answer me.

In the West End Collegiate Church basement, arrows pointed to meeting rooms for Overeaters Anonymous, Compulsive Workers Anonymous, Debtors Anonymous, and Cardiac Support. Apparently, dying people didn't have to be anonymous.

Ten decrepit people sat in a circle. Even the two Afro-Americans looked pale. I was sure I didn't look like that. They went around the circle whining. "Hi, I'm Francine, and I don't know how to tell my daughter that I am ready to let go and die…." "Hi, I'm Ralph, I keep having nightmares that I can't breathe…." "Hi, I'm Rachel. I watched my husband pass over three years ago, but nobody…." Rachel burst into tears. I passed my turn.

Afterward, waiting to hail a taxi, Cary said, "It was interesting to see people unburdening themselves like that." He was pathologically kind.

10

I didn't usually agree with my mother, but Nana was spot on when she blurted out, "That was a waste of time." A cab slid up next to us and from the back seat she went on, "A waste for me, I mean. For you, Andy, it's perfect. You'll feel all warm and snuggly after a few sessions."

I didn't respond to her sarcasm.

§§

I walked into the employee entrance at exactly 10:15. I'd been out for four days, and I still had a million sick days available because I never took time off.

I put my things in my locker, greeted Pearl at the locker next to mine, and went downstairs to the sales floor. Faith would be late, but as usual, Ryker beat me in. That was part of his manager mentality.

"Andy," he said with a smile, "it's about time you came back. I stole all your customers." His German accent was barely perceptible. Ryker was tall and built like an old swimmer. Next to him, my medium height looked short.

I did a mini-dance, happy to be back to work. "Anything new?"

"The Guerlain model quit. She said spritzing perfume was boring." He loaded the drawer under the showcase with Aqua de Parma. "The Modern Muse dusting powder arrived. I left a message for Ms. Montclair that it came."

I swept the sides of my hair back with my fingertips and said, "Then she'll be in this morning."

Ryker stood up. "You gave us a shock last week."

"Just some drama to spice things up on the floor." I took my client book out of my coat pocket.

"No, really, Andy. How are you feeling? Do I need to be ready to dial 911 again? I don't ever again want to see you lying on the floor comatose with your mouth gaping open." He grinned and went on, "You should have seen the audience that came over to watch. You were a celebrity and didn't even know it."

I cringed at the thought of people seeing me like that. I kept myself from asking if I had drooled. Instead, I put on a light tone to say, "No need to worry. I'm fine now."

I was back in my element. Ryker and Faith were as much my family as my daughter, mother, and Cary. The three of us marched in a syncopated rhythm around the counters, respecting boundaries and sharing jokes 5 days a week. Together, we put on a show for the customers, smiling and serving.

I'd been at Bergdorf's longer than Ryker and Faith, and I made more commissions than either of them. The products and clients were always changing, and that made every day stimulating. I was exceptionally talented at what I did. That is to say, at cajoling rich people into thinking they would be happier/prettier/sexier/admired if they bought such and such product.

I didn't lie. When I talked to them, I believed what I said. No two clients were alike, and the differences interested me.

Faith arrived, scampering in like a bunny just before the opening buzzer, as always. She hugged me. "I was so worried. I almost had a heart attack myself, seeing you on the floor like that."

In between customers, Ryker stocked and organized, I called my faithful clients, and Faith scooted around the floor to ask her friends in other departments about sales and markdowns.

By noon, I was exhausted. I kept my sales persona pasted on my face, but I signaled to Ryker that I was going on a lunch break. In the employee cafeteria, I sank into a chair by the window, too tired to go through the food line. I hadn't expected to feel worn out so early.

I propped my chin on my hand and closed my eyes. Ten minutes later, I woke up with a start when Brian from Men's Shoes touched me on the shoulder. "Glad to see you, Andy. I heard what happened."

I shooed him off with a lie, "I'm fine. It was just an excuse for a trip to Hawaii." We laughed, and he told me about the Ferragamo sale in the Men's Store. I stood up and got some fried cod, French fries, and apple cobbler to fortify me for the afternoon.

On my way back to the perfume department, I swung by the jewelry counter on the main floor.

"Hey, Andy," Frank Bryson said to me. "Are you ready to buy the ring?"

"Not today. But I could use a lift. Can I try it on?"

"I heard you were carted off to the hospital. You're okay now?"

I nodded without explaining while Frank unlocked the case and took out a Jorge Adeler 18k gold ring. It flaunted a Greek coin minted around 230 B.C. that featured the son of Poseidon.

Frank slipped the ring on my left hand. "Size 10. It's perfect on you. Very handsome."

Silently, I agreed. I hadn't worn a ring since my divorce eleven years back. I'd had my eye on this ring for over a year, but with a price tag of $5,470, Frank figured I was window-shopping. With my store discount, it would cost me just over $4,000.

Frank pulled out another ring with a different ancient coin. "You'd look good in this one too, Andy."

"It's Neptune, right?" I already knew the answer.

"Right," Frank smiled persuasively. "A little more expensive but gorgeous."

I knew the Neptune ring was $7,980. I had tried it on several months back. "But the coin's not dated," I noted.

Frank replied, "That's true," and he reluctantly returned the ring to the case.

I slid off the son of Poseidon ring and handed it back. "Is business holding up?" I asked him.

He gave the BG party line answer: "Never better."

I smiled and said, "Come downstairs today, and I'll load you up with fragrance samples."

§§

Behind the counter again, I considered asking Ryker if I could bring in a bar stool to sit on, only when I wasn't waiting on someone. It was strictly forbidden for the sales staff to sit, but I knew management would make an exception for me because I was special, and I'd argue that I was fragile after the heart attack.

I decided to tell Ryker family updates instead: "My mother keeps advising Chloé about her boyfriend George. 'Don't let him move in with you,' Nana says. 'I couldn't haven't stayed with Cary for 37 years if we'd lived together,' she says. As if living in the apartment next door is living apart. But for once, I agree with her. George isn't good enough for Chloé."

"What's he do?" Faith asked. She was the gossip manager of our little group.

I harrumphed and said, "He's a professional jackass."

Faith rolled her eyes, so I was more specific, "He's an agent for voice-over actors who do radio ads. He does all his work from his home on the computer. He probably wears pajamas all day."

"Or he just sits at his desk naked," Ryker laughed.

I cringed at the vision of George nude.

"But that's a solid job. Agents make good money," Faith said.

I had seen George enough to know that he was far from rich. "He's a dirtbag. But my ex-wife is celebrating the guy moving in with Chloé. I can imagine her motherly advice." I switched to a shrill voice, "'A man is like a big diamond, honey. You'll love having him around all the time.'" I grunted. "Like she knows, divorced eleven years and still moving from man to man."

We interrupted the conversation when a trio of customers approached.

At 3:20, I said to Ryker, "I'm going to take a break if it's okay. Ms. Montclair hasn't come in yet. Buzz me if she shows up."

I stood up straight until I reached the stockroom where I lowered myself onto a box and tried to breathe without panting. A few days off from standing up all day, and I was a wreck. I pulled out my client book and called six customers before I felt like I had enough energy to go back to the counter.

35 minutes before closing, I spotted a familiar form. "Oh! Ms. Montclair, what a pleasure to see you." I went around the counter to take her hand in both of mine. I didn't kiss it, but I held it as if I wanted to. "It's definitely been too long. How are your grandchildren? Ah, Henry is the boy, but tell me the girl's name again?"

Ms. Montclair bubbled over with tales about Henry and Faye and the trip they took together to the Maldives. I led her to the counter, and she looked at me sideways over her tortoise-shell glasses to whisper, "What do you have

17

that's out of the ordinary, Andy. I'm giving a small cocktail party tomorrow, and I want to smell extraordinary."

I wiggled my eyebrows at her.

"I know that mischievous look," she laughed.

"You can read me better than anyone," I said, leading her to the end of the counter. I reached into the cabinet and brought out a crystal flagon. "Shalini," I whispered back to her as if we were conspiring. I picked up a tester from the counter, sprayed the air lightly, and lifted the back of my hand through the mist; then I held my hand eight inches from Ms. Montclair's nose. "It has tuberose absolute and sandalwood. I know they're your favorites."

The silver haired woman closed her eyes, sniffed, and mocked a swoon. Opening her eyes slowly, she added, "And the Lalique bottle is exquisite."

"It's called 'Le Coquillage.' You can add it to your collection," I said.

"Is the bottle signed?"

I nodded, "Of course: hand-poured, numbered, and signed by Shalini. I have the fragrance in a purse spray too."

Ms. Montclair beamed happily. "Here's my card. I want both."

"Would you like a spritz from the tester to enjoy on your way home?" I offered.

As I rang up the sale, we chatted about the list of 100 people coming to her small cocktail party. Ms. Montclair blew me a kiss as she walked away.

18

Ryker came over and whispered to me, "That was a lot better than an Estee Lauder body powder."

Faith peeked in the cash drawer at the receipt. "You dog. Five minutes before closing and you make a $3,400 sale." She shook her head in admiration and left to go to her locker.

I walked out with Ryker. "If I'm a few minutes late tomorrow morning, it's because I have an appointment at Mount Sinai."

Ryker patted me on the shoulder and said, "No problem, Andy. It's good to have you back. The perfume counter is dull without you."

§§

"You went to work yesterday?" Ponytail asked me.

I nodded. We were in his Mount Sinai office. It was plain, but had a good-looking bookshelf covering the wall opposite the window. An exam table squeezed itself into one corner and various equipment filled the other corner. My chair was covered in grey linen. His desk was maple. Maybe cherry.

"How was it?" he asked.

"I made a few good sales."

"I mean, physically. Did you feel okay? Did you stay the whole day?" He stood up before I could answer, walked around his desk, and put his stethoscope to my heart.

"Stand up," he commanded. "Lift your arms." He tapped my back and listened again.

"Come over here, Mr. Brown," he said, pointing to the scales next to the window.

I rolled my eyes. The guy wasn't even a doctor, and he was ordering me around like a jail guard. "Is this really necessary?" I asked, hoping my haughty attitude came through.

Ponytail smiled without showing any teeth. "Yes," he answered without explaining.

I stepped on the scale with digital numbers flashing on a screen at waist level.

20

Ponytail wrote with a metal pen on an electronic tablet, then checked my height on the yardstick on the wall.

"You can sit down again," he declared. He wrapped my arm with a blood pressure contraption, took my pulse, then my temperature.

Sinking into his chair, he jotted more hieroglyphs in his tablet. From behind his desk, Ponytail sounded like a parent lecturing a child, "Do you know how much you weigh, Mr. Brown?"

"I saw the reading the same as you," I answered. I hoped I sounded self-righteous and not defensive.

"268 pounds. And you're 5' 9 ½". I want you to repeat those numbers out loud."

I sat up straight to say, "I've always been a big man."

Ponytail looked at his hands, then looked up at me. "You are not a big man, Mr. Brown. You are obese. Dangerously obese."

"My weight doesn't stop me from doing anything I want." I paused. "And that includes having sex." I didn't say how long it had been since I'd had a roll in the hay, or even been on a date, but that had nothing to do with my size.

The tall, young, ponytailed cardiac nurse practitioner looked to the side, then to the other side, up to the ceiling, and back at me, as if he'd decided what to say. "I met your daughter."

I nodded and said, "Chloé, she's lovely, and a great physical therapist."

21

"Your mother gave me your medical history."

"Yes, Nanette Brown. Acclaimed painter."

"I'm sure they both love you."

They loved me. I knew that. I steeled myself for him to do the "don't let them lose someone they love" spiel.

But he surprised me. "So why have they let you get this fat?"

"You can't say that. You're a medical professional. My weight isn't their responsibility, and you know it. I'm happy and healthy, and that's enough for them."

"Except you're not healthy."

"It's been entertaining to meet with you." I stood up to leave without extending my hand for a shake.

"Oh, stop the drama and listen to me," he said and pointed to the chair.

I sat but decided I might not listen. I was 52 years old. I would never be in shape, and I knew it.

"I have 3 prescriptions for you."

He went on, as if I hadn't smirked. "Number 1: Keep taking your heart medicines."

I figured I could and would do that one, but I didn't give him the satisfaction of saying so.

"Where do you live?" he asked.

"Amsterdam and 69th Street," I answered.

"And where do you work?"

With a hint of pride that I couldn't hide, I said, "Bergdorf Goodman."

"Good," he said, as if I had gotten the answer correct. "Number 2: Walk to and from work every day. Tomorrow walk halfway in each direction, then take the bus. But starting next week, walk the entire distance, no matter what the weather."

The guy was dreaming. Walk to Bergdorf's in the rain? I'd have to completely re-dress when I arrived to be halfway presentable for my clients.

"And your number 3 is you want me to eat nothing but raw carrots and grapefruits," I sniggered.

"No. Number 3: Tell a secret each week."

I let out a huff of air. "Don't be ridiculous. I don't have secrets."

Ponytail laughed like he'd seen a dog talking French. "We all have secrets. I'm betting that you're fat because you hide lots of secrets."

I crossed my arms over my chest and fumed with rage at the asshole across the desk from me. First he called me fat, and then he accused me of being dishonest. His behavior was not acceptable.

"Here's my prediction, Mr. Brown. When you tell a secret, you'll lose 5 pounds. A secret a week, 5 pounds a week."

"Don't be stupid. That's impossible." It was the nicest of the things I wanted to say to him.

"Mr. Brown, fat is not necessarily a bad thing. Some people are fat and healthy. Some are fat by nature or by heredity. But that's not your case. I want you to lose 100 pounds, and my best suggestion to you is to put your secrets on the table and stop carrying them around."

"So you think you're a shrink now?" I let my sarcasm ooze over the words.

He came back at me with his own dose of sarcasm, "You can ride 2 ½ hours a day on a stationary bike if you prefer." He paused, as if he knew that bicycle exercise was a ridiculous suggestion. "100 pounds," he repeated.

Ponytail was asking me to lose almost half of myself in six months. I hated him. I looked at the name plate on his desk: Bradley Matthews, APRN, CVRN, MSN, DNP.

I refused to fall prey to all those letters. He was Mr. Matthews, and I wouldn't give him the satisfaction of saying his name. I looked at my watch. Already 10:07.

He stood up and walked to the office door. "Yes, it's time for you to leave."

What an arrogant bastard! I didn't budge from my chair, to spite him. "You're talking six months of intensive weight loss. That can't be healthy for me."

He snickered and asked, "How was cardiac group therapy?"

I wasn't going back for another meeting with those whiners, and it sounded like he already knew it. I stayed silent.

He opened the door and said, "Prove me wrong about the secrets."

I swung around in my chair to face him. "Why in the world would you want to hear my secrets?"

"Oh, don't tell them to me, Mr. Brown. I don't want to hear about your life. Anyone else will do, but be careful who you pick. Avoid people who might ridicule you or blackmail you."

I shook my head. There was no communicating with this egomaniac. I stood up and walked past him through the doorway.

"I expect to see you here at next week's check-up. Same time, same place," he called after me.

Yeah, right, I thought.

§§

I took the M5 bus home from work. As usual, I'd had a successful day at Bergdorf Goodman, but my mind kept flashing back to dumbass Ponytail standing at his door asking me to leave his office. I sat up straighter in my seat. I growled deep in my throat, and the lady sitting next to me tensed up. At the Columbus Circle and 8th Avenue stop, I crawled over her and got off the bus.

Usually I got off at Broadway and 68th Street. But the sun was out; the temperature was 61° at 7:10 p.m. It was only 10 blocks to my apartment, and the stroll home would let me enjoy the bustle around Lincoln Center. I could make it to Bread's Bakery before they closed and buy a chocolate babka to take to Nana and Cary's tonight for the party.

I chuckled and corrected myself: to *Cary's* tonight. They had been partners since my father died 37 years ago and had never lived together. That was *Nana's* idea, of course. Her favorite defense of her living situation was to quote Katherine Hepburn, "Sometimes I wonder if men and women really suit each other. Perhaps they should live next door and just visit now and then."

And of course, if I made a comment about the two adjacent apartments, she'd raise an eyebrow and say, "And who are you, Mr. Divorcé, to criticize our relationship?"

In front of Target on Broadway, I paused to catch my breath. Bread's Bakery was only 2 more blocks.

I'd been on my feet all day at Bergdorf's, other than a couple of breaks, so I sat down on a bench in front of Juilliard to rest.

"Andy, 5 more blocks to go," I said out loud to myself and stood up.

15 minutes later, I'd never been so happy to step inside my building's elevator and push the button to the 6th floor. The damn heart attack was making me weak.

I took off my suit coat, set my wallet on the dresser, put all my change in the blue crystal vase, and slipped off my loafers.

From a prone position on the couch, I called my mother. "I'm not going to make it to the party tonight. I just got home, and I'm tired."

There was a pause on the line, like she was thinking; then the voice crackled, "Of course you're tired, Andy. You just had a heart attack. But if you can go to work, you can come here. I'll hold dinner until 8:30."

It was my turn to pause. Arguing with Nana was not easy, even when I was full of energy. "Let me talk to Cary," I said.

"He's here waiting for you," Nana answered, with a pretend smile in her tone. "Take a taxi," she said, and the connection went dead.

§§

I forgot the chocolate babka and had to go back upstairs to get it. By the time I hailed a cab and arrived at 98th Street, it was 8:40.

On the 16th floor, Chloé stood in the open doorway of Cary's apartment, her red frames on her nose and her cropped hair sticking out in various directions. Blue wagged at her side. "Daddy," she grinned and hugged me, "You're exactly on time." She was a great liar.

I handed her the babka and went into the dining room to greet everyone. When I said hello to George, an imaginary picture of him sitting at his desk naked almost blinded me. I'd have to tell Ryker that the young man sat at the table with clothes on, a blue shirt and blue jeans.

Cary was the cook of the Nanette/Cary partnership, and the smells from the kitchen were Italian, not French. He came to the dining room door and waved at me with a wooden spoon. I greeted him by putting a small BG bag on the table at his place.

"Gifts after dinner," Nana said with a happy glint in her eyes. She pointed to a chair for me to sit down and looked at her watch to emphasize my tardiness.

I rebounded with, "I'm glad to see you too, Nana."

"It wouldn't be a party without you, Andy. Are you drinking?" Without me answering, she told George, "Pour my son some wine. I read that wine's good for a man with stents."

Wine sounded great. I finished a glass of red by the time Cary carried in a platter and sat down, saying, "Will you serve the cannelloni, George? You're in charge of the salad, Chloé. You don't mind shaving the parmesan for me, I hope?"

"Not a problem, Cary, as long as I can accidently drop a little cheese on the floor for you-know-who." Chloé winked at the giant silver poodle weaving around her legs.

The oohs and ahhs filled the dining room when the clan started eating.

"Where did you learn to cook like this, Cary?" George asked.

"Every boy in France learns to cook from his mother," Cary smiled. "Plus, I worked in the kitchen on a Mediterranean cruise ship every summer during University. That helped."

I envied his debonaire accent.

"Then you came to the U.S.?" George pushed.

"More wine, please," Cary asked, holding his glass out to my mother. He took a sip and said, "I was a banker with PNB Paribas in Lyon, then Paris, and finally was transferred to New York."

Nana wiped the red sauce from her lip and said, "I banked at J.P. Morgan, but I managed to meet Cary at an exhibition in Soho. Lucky for me."

I'd heard the story before. Cary showed up at the Ronald Feldman Gallery because his lady friend of the moment wanted to see Nanette Brown's works, her first exhibition since my father had died. When she was introduced to Cary Lambert, my mother wrote a note on one of her business cards and handed it to him. It wasn't until the next day that Cary read it: "To the tall handsome man, 212-551-6743. Nanette B."

On that night at the gallery, Nana had been a widow for less than six months. Apparently she was ready to come out of mourning, and apparently, it wasn't easy to say No to an audacious painter, because Cary called her.

Cary blushed, but George didn't ask for the juicy details. Instead, my daughter's boyfriend asked my mother, "How many paintings have you done?"

It used to flatter Nana when people asked about her work. Now, at 73 years old, she almost yawned as she answered, "An incalculable number. It's as if I live with a brush in my hand."

George kept on, asking where he could see the paintings and how she got her ideas. Cary and Chloé answered for her while Nana soaked up the sauce on her plate with bread and finished her wine.

"Let's have dessert in the living room," Nana said. "Fix me a sherry, Cary darling."

Cary stood up. My god, he was still tall at 70 years old, and his white hair rolled back from his forehead in waves. "No, sweetheart. You are going to have port, like me and Andy. Chloé can have whatever she wants. You too, George."

Chloé grinned. "I'll bring the desserts, and the drinks too. You two go in and sit down with Blue." She tipped her head to me and George to follow her to the kitchen.

George turned around 360° in the kitchen. "This is a great apartment. How many bedrooms is it?"

"These pre-war buildings were built for comfort," I answered him. "It's got four bedrooms, plus the kitchen, dining room and living room, and two giant bathrooms. Cary sleeps in one bedroom, uses one as a library, another as an office, and then there's a guest room."

"Nana's apartment next door is the mirror image of this one but in reverse," Chloé explained, before she went on in a whisper: "Listen, we're going to ignore what Cary told us. Tonight, it's champagne with the caramel mousse. Daddy, take out five dessert cups from the fridge. Put one on each plate, and a slice of your babka on the side. Cary's has to have a candle."

"Not 70 candles?" I teased.

She pushed her glasses up on her nose and pulled five champagne flutes out of the cabinet.

"Did they live next door to each other before they got together?" George asked.

Chloé smiled. "Their story could be a movie. From what I've heard over the years, Nana lived in the apartment next door with her husband and my father."

I butted in with, "My dad died before Chloé was born."

"Nana had been a widow for a couple of months when this apartment was sold to 'some foreigner'." Her laugh tinkled through the kitchen. "Apparently, she saw glimpses of the new neighbor a few times before she met him at the exhibition."

"So, Chloé tells me you two are moving in together," I said to George.

"Yeah, it'll be great. I live on the East Side. Being over here with her will be like paradise."

"Her place is nothing like Cary's," I said, like a warning, as if he didn't already know where my daughter lived.

"No, but it's bigger than his studio," Chloé laughed, and I pressed my lips together.

Chloé checked the plates and announced we were ready.

I carried the dessert tray with five plates and one flickering candle, George had the drink tray, and Chloé held the napkins and forks, while we paraded into the living room singing *Happy Birthday*.

Blue barked and Nana kissed Cary's cheek. She whispered in his ear, loud enough for me to hear, "You only turn 70 once, my love." Maybe if I had Cary's accent, someone would adore me like that.

§§

I got half-way through the caramel mousse and felt a yawn working its way up to my mouth. I leaned back in my easy chair and pretended to be full, so I could cover my mouth with the napkin. Well, I deserved to be tired. It had been a long day.

"Do you not like the champagne, Andy?" Cary asked, taking note of my full glass on the coffee table.

Instead of answering him, I stood up and asked if anyone else wanted seltzer. I had to move, or I'd fall asleep. There were no takers.

"Time for presents," Chloé chirped and pointed to the sacks on the lamp table. "Mine is the green bag. It's from George too."

My daughter, always making nice. I'd bet my next paycheck that George had nothing to do with Chloé's gift.

Cary opened the green sack and pushed through blue tissue paper to find a white box. "Oh, they're splendid," he said, pulling out a silver cufflink. He half-rose to lean over and give Chloé's cheek a kiss. Then he was nicer than I would have been and reached out to shake George's hand. "Thank you. Thank you both."

"You're the only man I know who wears cufflinks, Cary," Chloé said. "I ordered the francs from the Monnaie de Paris -- they're from 1992 -- and I had them set into cufflinks. I hope you like them."

"I recognize the francs. They're fabulous, just like you, Chloé."

She sat tall like she was proud of herself.

"The Bergdorf Goodman bag, I imagine that's from you, Andy," Cary said with a smile.

"It's from Paris too," I said, watching him pull out the bottle of Bois Mystique eau de parfum.

Cary spritzed the air in front of him and raised his nose. "Ah, woody. Very nice." He spritzed again, captured the mist on his hand, and put it on his neck. "What do you think, my love?" When Nana sniffed and swooned against him, he announced, "It's very effective. Thank you, Andy."

"Do you get colognes for free from the store, Andy?" George asked. I didn't want him to call me 'Andy.' I thought 'Mr. Brown' would be more respectful for a girlfriend's father, but the dickhead's manners were not in my control.

I tried to answer in my professional voice, "No. We get discounts, and sometimes there are extra testers we can have."

"An abundance of fragrance is one of the things I love about my son," Nana said. "I always have perfume and samples galore." She leaned over, patted my knee, and said lightly, "One of the *many* things I love about you, son."

It happened like that. I was getting in the groove of resenting and disliking Nanette Brown's bossiness and disdain when she popped my bubble with a sweet remark, seemingly sincere and warm. I felt myself flush.

34

George broke the spell. "It's lucky I don't work at a place like Bergdorf Goodman. I think I'd be tempted to slip diamond bracelets in my pocket at closing time. Or walk out wearing a cashmere sweater I 'forgot' to pay for."

I nodded. "Yes, stealing is a potential hazard." Instead of saying something rude to George, I settled for, "When I was a child, I used to steal my father's loose change from the top of his highboy. Luckily, I grew up."

Nana swung toward me, "You did that?"

I hadn't meant to say what I'd said. I'd kept my childhood habit a secret for more than 40 years, and now I was probably in trouble, as if I were still 10 years old.

Nana raved on, "I never knew you did that, Andy. I used to steal the bills from Tom's highboy. Well, not all of them. Only the $1's and $5's. Sometimes a $10."

I couldn't believe it. My mother stealing from my father?

She laughed. "I didn't need the money. It just seemed like the thing to do. Looking back, I suppose your father knew what I was doing. He was probably onto your pilfering too." Cary put his arm around her, and she added innocently, "I've never stolen from you, darling."

He smirked and kept quiet.

"It must be hereditary," Chloé said. "When I started smoking cigarettes at 16, I bought them with money from your dresser, Daddy."

"You smoked cigarettes?!" I demanded.

"Only in the 10th and 11th grades with Lucy Freeman."

35

"So, I'm surrounded by thieves," George laughed. It was as if he wanted to be part of the happy gang. Chloé laughed of course.

I looked at my daughter with her spiky hair and happy expression and found a second wind, as if the workday had been erased.

"One more present, Cary," Chloé chirped. "We want to see you open Nana's gift."

Cary fished a flat box out of the sack my mother handed to him. "Oh, Nanette. It's very nice," he said, looking at the wallet inside.

I nodded in approval, "Giorgi Armani, Italian."

Nana stopped Cary from putting an appreciative kiss on her check. "That's not the gift," she said. "Open the billfold."

"Nana, he doesn't need $100 bills. Save those for me," Chloé joked.

"No," Cary disagreed, chuckling. "$100's are good for me too." He took the wallet out of the flat box and opened it. "Ah, the real gift." He stared at the open wallet for several seconds before he embraced Nanette. "Yes, the real gift. Thank you, my dear, for everything." Then he passed the open wallet to Chloé.

"Ah, Nana," she crooned and showed me the photo inside the wallet, a picture of my mother and Cary standing together on the front of the Staten Island Ferry in brilliant sunlight, with the Freedom Tower rising behind them.

"In my old wallet, I carry a picture of us on the ferry with the Twin Towers behind us." Cary tightened his arm around Nana's shoulders, remembering. "This one is better."

George put his arm around Chloé's shoulders too.

"I have a request," Nana said. She was using her command voice, not her do-me-a-favor voice. We all sat at attention. "George, walk Blue around the block for her evening pee."

I would have gotten a kick out of it if George had tried to say No. But no such luck. Apparently, he knew who was boss and left with the big grey poodle on leash.

"I wanted a family moment," Nana said, "so Andy could celebrate his father – yes, since you were 15, Cary has served as your father."

"Oh my god," Cary cried with a smile. "Do we have to say how many years that has been?"

It didn't take me more than two seconds to calculate my 52 years minus 15, but I kept quiet for Cary's sake.

Nana went on, "And for Chloé to adore her grandfather in private."

My daughter moved to the arm of the couch and kissed Cary on the cheek. "Nana's right," she said. "You are a treasure."

I nodded my agreement.

Cary blushed and said in a choked up voice, "You're the treasure, my dear." He patted her arm. "Whatever you do, I want you to be healthy and happy." He wiped his eyes with the back of his hand. "You too, Andy."

Nana sniffed with an edge of contempt, "They'd both be healthy and happy if they listened to me more often."

Chloé laughed and shifted to the other side of the couch, "You're a treasure too, Nana."

"You're sure about this cohabitating thing you're planning?" Nana asked. "You've noticed that George is short, barely taller than you. You'll never be able to wear high heels."

"Nana, you're so funny. He's the same height as Daddy."

"That's what I mean," Nana said. "Short."

I rolled my eyes.

Chloé glanced at me over the red frames of her glasses and asked, "Do you want coffee?"

"Not me," I answered. "It's time I get home. I work tomorrow, you know."

"Don't overdo," Nana warned. "I don't want to spend more time in the hospital."

Chloé jumped up and planted a kiss on my cheek. "I'll talk to you soon, Daddy. I had fun tonight." My daughter always had fun.

"Good food, wine, champagne, and a good night's sleep. That sounds like an excellent prescription," Cary said. "Let me walk you out, Andy."

George was coming out of the elevator when Cary opened the door. "George, do me a favor. Walk to Broadway and hail a cab for Andy."

I intervened with, "Oh, that's not necessary."

Cary winked at me, "Oh yes, Father knows best. Blue can take one last sniff for the night."

George was grumbling when he pushed the elevator button. Me too. But Blue wagged her tail.

Broadway was within sight when Blue decided to stop and take a crap. George leaned over to clean up; then flipping the poop bag closed, he said, "Giant shit. Giant dog. But Cary's giant apartment, that's really something."

I could ignore his limited vocabulary, but the cretin should be more respectful toward Cary and call him *Mr. Lambert.* I had my mouth open to tell him, when George raised his hand and said, "Here's a taxi for you, Andy." The cab stopped next to us, and George opened the backseat door.

I looked at him holding a crap bag and said simply, "Goodnight, George," giving him my best smile, displaying my whitened teeth to full advantage in the moonlight.

§§

Again, I was early for my Mount Sinai appointment. Ponytail's office door was open, and I went in to explore before the pushy nurse-boy arrived. His bookshelves were full of medical books, Braunwald's Heart Disease volumes 1 and 2, Cardiac Valvular Medicine, Encyclopedia of Cardiovascular Research and Medicine, Sports Cardiology - Care of the Athletic Heart from the Clinic to the Sideline, Wasserman & Whipp's Principles of Exercise Testing and Interpretation, Cardiac Catheterization and Coronary Intervention. I understood the titles, but the initials after the authors' names were impossible: FACC, FESC, FAPSC, ACVC, ESC, MPH. Whatever happened to M.D.?

Ponytail had a photo on his desk of a boy about 10 years old, a few file folders, a half-full coffee cup, and a big jar of matchbooks from restaurants. I interpreted each item: married and divorced with one child, not many patients today, called away by a real doctor before he could finish his coffee, and apparently this stupid health care professional smoked cigarettes. Also, he ate out a lot, so he didn't know how to cook.

His window was tiny, showing a sliver of the Hudson River. I ignored the stationary bicycle next to the medical sink and focused on a metal cabinet which I figured was full of medicines and needles and other paraphernalia.

"Are you searching for opioids?" a voice said close to my ear, making me jump. I recovered quickly enough to lie, "Hello. I just arrived and was making my way to the chair," which I did immediately and sat down.

"Thank you for being on time, Mr. Brown," Ponytail said. "Let's get started with your blood pressure," and he put the inflatable band around my arm. My PB was probably high after the stress of being caught examining his office.

He listened to my heart, front and back, took my pulse, and pointed me to the scales.

"262," he announced, recording my weight on his tablet.

He pointed again, this time to the chair for me to sit down. From behind his desk, "How do you feel, Mr. Brown?"

"So my heart is still beating?" I asked in return.

"Your heart is beating." He folded his hands on his desk. "How did your week go? Did you have any fatigue? Was work tiring? Did you walk to and from work like I suggested? Any reaction to the medications? In other words, how do you feel, Mr. Brown?"

I smirked at his smart-aleck bedside manner. "I feel fine. I am always tired after a lucrative sales day. I walked to and from work except Wednesday. I came here on foot this morning. How about you? How do you feel?" I thought I matched his smart-aleck tone rather well.

I thought I saw his upper lip twitch as if he wanted to smile. No, I was imagining it.

"Your blood pressure is 132/88. That's good. You're responding to the medication well, it seems. And you've lost weight."

I pursed my lips together. I wasn't going to mention the chocolate chip ice cream I'd had on top on a slice of banana cake at lunch yesterday. Or the bottle of red wine Ryker and I shared after work Friday night. Or any of my other pleasures. "So you're not going to chain me to the Ketogenic diet?"

"So, you're familiar with popular regimens for losing weight? Have you tried Volumetrics? Or Probiotics?"

"I've told you, I've always been a big man. I don't do diets."

"And I didn't ask you to do diets, did I? All I asked is that you tell secrets. Remember?"

I growled low in my throat, too low for him to hear, and leaned forward with my palms on his desk. "And we both know that telling secrets is bullshit. First, it's good to have a private life, and second, it has nothing to do with my weight."

"But you lost 6 pounds this past week. How do you explain that? You told a secret. Right?"

I was not going to admit the slip I made at Cary's birthday party when I mentioned the money I used to steal from my father's chest-of-drawers. Besides, it turned out that Nana did the same thing. There was no reason not to talk about it after all these years, so it wasn't like telling a secret.

I lifted my chin and said knowingly, "I imagine all patients lose weight after having heart attacks and operations."

Ponytail smiled. In fact, he had rather good teeth, incisors somewhat pointed, but other than that, good dental presentation. He should smile more often.

"My patients? Yes, they all lose weight." He dropped the smile. "I hope you walk from here to work, and I will see you next week." He stood up, walked around his desk, and opened the door.

In my opinion, Ponytail nurse didn't do much to earn his living.

I twisted around in the chair. "I was thinking about the stents. What can I expect in the future? Will they have to put in more stents? It's just like a straw on the inside of an artery, right? To let the blood flow?"

He didn't go back to his desk. Instead Ponytail pulled a chair up next to mine. "The stent is exactly like a straw in a vein or artery. As long as you don't have any more blockages, you won't need more stents." He reached for the framed photo on his desk and handed it to me. "That's Ted Percy. He was my first patient 5 years ago. He had a heart defect that Maggie Park – she's *your* surgeon – a defect that Dr. Park fixed with three stents when the boy was 8 years old. Today, he's on a soccer team that's leading the middle-school city league. Ted and I have an appointment here once a month."

"I thought the picture was your son."

"Not married, and no children," Ponytail said. He leaned toward me. "You can live a long time, Mr. Brown, if you do things right."

§§

I rang at Nana's apartment and heard Blue barking. The dog was a better doorbell than the buzzer on the doorframe.

Cary opened the door with a big smile, holding a box of chocolates, looking dapper in a linen shirt and khaki slacks. "I invited a friend to go with us," he announced. "He'll meet us on the sidewalk."

Blue came out of the apartment and sniffed the crotch of my navy slacks. "Yes, Blue, it's me," I said.

Nana followed the dog out of the apartment, kissed me on the check, and straightened my lavender tie.

"Chloé and George are meeting us downstairs," I told her.

She told the giant poodle, "Blue, go inside. We'll be back," and she locked the door.

On the sidewalk, a man wearing a navy blazer over a pale blue t-shirt came up to Cary.

Cary made the introductions, "Ned Lewis, meet Nanette Brown, and her son Andy. Ned's a friend from the gym."

I reached out to shake his hand and said, "Cary loves that gym. Nana tells me if he's not home, then he's either at the gym or Whole Foods."

Ned patted Cary on the shoulder. "I see him at Crunch every morning."

My mother looked Ned up and down. He was 30-ish, short blond hair, and built like a tennis star. "Yes, you're in shape," she said definitively. Cary was the 70-year-old version of the same type. I tamped down my jealousy.

"Ned lives in the building across the street," Cary told us. "I told Nicole he'd fit in the group without any problem."

Chloé approached from Broadway. "Hello everyone," she said, making the rounds to kiss me, Cary, and her grandmother. Then she announced, "George isn't coming. He apologized. He's on-line in the middle of a high stakes poker game and couldn't leave." She smiled, "But I'm here, ready for our adventure."

I didn't know where Chloé inherited her gentle character. A boyfriend cancelling because he was gambling? I would have been livid. Hell, I was livid. I took a breath and reminded myself that her private life was not my business.

Without fanfare, Cary introduced Chloé to the gym friend from across the street; then he took a lady on each arm, saying, "Onward!" That left me and Ned Lewis to follow.

We were too many for a taxi, and I imagined Nana and Chloé whispering about the "heart patient" who couldn't walk very far, so we loaded onto the M96 bus, transferred to the M11, and walked the last block to Central Park West and 64th Street. We headed into a building and went up to the fourth floor in a brass elevator. The hostess Nicole Fisher greeted us at the apartment door wearing an ankle-length white dress absolutely plain except for a big silver necklace at her neck.

"Welcome!" she said to Nana, kissing her on both cheeks. She squealed with pleasure when Cary gave her the box of chocolates. "You must be Chloé!" she added, giving more kisses to my daughter. "Nanette and Cary have told me stories about you. I am so glad you could come."

Chloé straightened her glasses and smiled, "It's wonderful to see the air show from your home, Ms. Fisher. Thank you for having me." She shook the hostess's hand warmly, the way her mother and grandmother had taught her from childhood. She'd gotten other lessons from me.

"Nicole. Call me Nicole," the elegant woman said. "Your grandmother has meant so much to me. She is a long-time friend. And the success of her work, you must be very proud."

"Yes. I'm lucky to have Nana." Chloé smiled, still holding the woman's hand.

"You've met my son Andy," my mother said, and I repeated the greeting ritual.

Then it was Ned's turn. Cary made the introduction, "My pal from Crunch Gym, Ned Lewis. Tell Nicole what you do, Ned."

He took the hostess's hand lightly, "It's a pleasure to meet you."

"And what do you do, Mr. Ned Lewis?" Nicole pressed.

"I work in administration for New York City Ballet."

"Oh how exciting, Ned. We'll have to meet up before a performance. Come in, come in to meet the others," Nicole Fisher said. "I live by myself, since my husband died, but Manhattan is a small town. I never feel alone."

I nodded with a smile. It was a "small town" where a single person lived in an eight room apartment worth several million dollars.

Passing through the living room and dining room, I spotted two of Nana's paintings hanging in prominent places, one over the couch, and the other between two of the French doors opening onto the terrace. I tipped my head toward them for Chloé to look, but I didn't need to. She recognized her grandmother's work as quickly as I did. Nanette Brown's works were easy to identify with their abstract streaks.

We joined eight people gathered on the long terrace overlooking Central Park. All the French doors were open, so that the living room and kitchen seemed to flow out to the trees. The terrace table was covered with plates of pastries, fruits, and cheeses. The guests chatted and sipped bloody Mary's, gin and tonics, daiquiris, or seltzer with fresh mint. Below, people were filling the sidewalk and streaming into the park.

Without announcement, the show began. To the left, from the direction of Columbia University, a single hot air balloon appeared, striped with blue, red and white. It rose and drifted south toward us, followed by a bright orange balloon, then one with red stars on a light blue background. We were at the perfect vantage point. On Nicole Fisher's terrace, we ahhh'ed and ohhh'ed each time another balloon floated up and over, circling and drifting, landing in the middle of the park. The pedestrians below clapped as loudly as we did.

Suddenly, eight fighter planes in a tight formation swooped low across the sky, trailing blue vapor behind. The show went on for twenty minutes with the airplanes weaving red, white, and blue vapor trails. A few minutes later, the hot air balloons lifted off going south.

"What a magnificent display!" Ned Lewis said, "Breath-taking! Thank you so much for this opportunity." Nana and Cary applauded. I congratulated Nicole for best show in town. Chloé laughed and said, "Encore!" Everyone on the terrace had something to say about the air display.

Three women in maid's uniforms came out carrying dishes, and we arranged ourselves at the terrace table for dinner. Nana sat next to me for the mussels, but when the pasta with artichoke sauce came out, she moved next to Cary. Chloé was between a retired art history professor and a photographer from Guatemala. I had a banker on my right who discussed 1980's jazz, saying his favorite was Miles Davis.

I spent the entire time with the tomato and avocado salad trying to convince him to reconsider Wayne Shorter. "I used to picture myself with a saxophone, and Shorter was my imaginary mentor. What a life that would have been." I drifted off into la-la land for an instant with the vision, then snapped back. I had never mentioned that daydream out loud.

A third wine was served with the chocolate cake topped with lemon sherbet, and the man opposite us joined the jazz argument. A vintner specializing in selling wine to yachts, he insisted Herbie Hancock was the best. "I always wanted to play the piano," he said. "I took lessons when I was a kid, five years of lessons, but I just didn't have any talent."

"You could have been Handcock's back-up," the banker said to him without irony.

I showed off my jazz expertise with, "Hancock and Shorter won a Grammy Award together for *Aung San Suu Kyi*. Do you remember it?"

"That was on the *1+1* album," the vintner said. "1995, wasn't it?"

"'97," I corrected with a smile and pushed away my cake half-eaten. That was when I noticed Chloé had changed her seat and was sitting next to Ned Lewis, talking intently about something I couldn't hear. The young man was nice looking. But who knew? He could be a bigger jerk than George.

Nana's hand covered Cary's next to her wine glass while she chatted with the guests about art and crime, movies and politics, as if she were the guest of honor. She spoke; people listened. She laughed; people laughed with her. She loved an audience. She should have been an actress instead of an artist, I thought.

Around 10:00, the long process of goodbyes began, everyone kissing, hugging and thanking.

Finally our crowd of five was back on Central Park West. "Ned, you and Chloé have to come home with us to have a coffee," Nana said.

"I'll go up with you as far as 86th. I have early patients tomorrow," Chloé said.

"Tomorrow's Sunday," I pushed her. "Come for coffee." I planned to lounge around all day the next day.

"Sorry, Daddy. I have to earn a living," she said with a smile.

"She's lucky to have work she likes," Cary said.

The M11 showed up and we climbed on.

Ned sat across the aisle from me and Chloé. "What kind of patient do you have tomorrow?" he asked her.

"She's a physical therapist," I answered for her.

Nana, next to Cary in the row behind us, jumped in the conversation, "Chloé works with the Hanger Clinic for Prosthetics in the mornings and Rugby New York in the afternoons."

Chloé managed to take over for herself, saying, "Nana and Daddy are my biggest supporters," she said. "I have private clients too. Tomorrow morning, I meet with a client who had a double mastectomy. We're working on re-developing her arm strength and coordination."

Ned nodded, "It must be challenging work. I never …."

Chloé stood up, cutting him off. "Here's my stop. Thanks for the spectacular air show and dinner, Nana and Cary. Daddy, I love you." She waved as she went down the bus steps. "Nice to meet you, Ned."

The transfer to the crosstown M96 was easy, and we trooped up to Nana's apartment. Blue met us at the door and followed us back inside. Nana's place was half the size of Nicole Fisher's, and was decorated opposite to Cary's twin apartment next door. It had pale rose walls, covered with paintings. Some of them were Nana's work, like the big piece in the living room: two horizontal slashes, orange and white, with a pink line skittering through the middle. She sometimes used other colors, of course. She even had one series where she used only purples, but her signature colors were orange and pink.

After my 52 years with Nana, I barely noticed her colors or the works by other artists. Cary was the same. But Ned couldn't sit down. He stood in the living room, slowing turning around, recognizing works by David Hockney, Willem de Kooning, Judy Chicago, Annie Leibovitz, Agnes Martin, Roy Lichtenstein, Louise Bourgeois, Yoko Ono, Cy Twombly, Laura Owens, and Andrew Wyeth.

"Sit down," Nana pushed him. "Cary will bring in coffee."

Ned stuttered, "These paintings? You...? Where did you...?

Nana cozied onto the couch next to Blue and slid her shoes off. "Years ago, I wanted to heat up my career, so I exchanged paintings with as many artists as I could find." She winked at him like a conspirator, "You know, lots of artists pass through New York City. It was a great way to spread my work around."

"The by-product was this collection she accumulated," Cary added, coming in with a tray of cups and a carafe of coffee. "The modern art contrasts well with the old fashioned furniture, don't you think?"

Ned nodded and sat down in an easy chair covered in Gingham. "Very Americana," he said sweetly.

"Years ago, Nanette turned the two back rooms into one big studio," Cary said. "You can see the bedrooms and kitchen if you want, but no one goes in the studio."

"Except you, my darling," Nana said with a wink.

I was impressed with Cary's friend. It wasn't everyone who walked into Nana's apartment and realized she was more than a retired lady living on a fixed income. She splurged on things for Chloé; otherwise, she was frugal to the point of being tight. Everything she had was invested in well-insured fine art.

I crossed my legs and took a sip of my coffee. "You said you work at the New York City Ballet," I said to Ned.

"Usually I say I'm in administration. It's less intimidating than telling the truth."

"Which is?" Nana asked.

"I'm the Director of Development for the Ballet."

"Development," I repeated. "You mean fundraising."

He nodded. "I was the head of Major Gifts at Symphony Space until NYCB approached me last year."

"So you ask people for money," I said with an edge of sarcasm.

He smirked and replied, "I believe you are a salesperson at Bergdorf Goodman?"

Nana laughed out loud, "Touché, Ned. Yes, my darling son also asks people for money."

"And Andy is very good at what he does," Cary added, as if he were a proud father.

"I'm sure he is," Ned conceded. "And if you like ballet, Andy, I'll be happy to comp you tickets to some performances, if you promise to use them yourself and not give them to your customers."

"I have a subscription for Cary and me," Nana said. "But I'm sure Chloé would love tickets too, whenever possible."

"Done," Ned toasted Nana with his coffee cup.

"Nana, Cary, the coffee was superb as usual, but it's time for me to get home." No one moved except Blue when I stood up.

§§

This week, Ponytail was waiting for me in his office. He did his routine, blood pressure, pulse, stethoscope, a quick sonogram of my neck, and weight.

"256 pounds," he said with a smirk when he sat down.

I did not reply. I'd seen the scale's readout.

"Clearly, you are unburdening yourself," Ponytail said, jotting notes on his tablet.

"I had a good week," I said, letting condescension bubble up through my tone.

He nodded. "You lost 6 pounds in seven days. You must have told the police about the heist you did at the Metropolitan Museum to lose so much weight in seven days."

I looked at Ponytail in confusion.

"That's a joke," he said, paused when I didn't react, then changed the subject, "I've been thinking about art, ever since I realized that your mother, the woman I met when your stents were inserted, your mother is Nanette Brown." He waited for my reaction. "The artist?"

I'd heard it a million times, "Oh your mother, your famous mother, she's so wonderful, you're so lucky," and on and on. "Yes, the artist," I confirmed.

"Do you paint?" he asked, leaning back in his chair.

"Is this part of your weekly exam?" I shot back.

"I like knowing about my patients."

"You know where I work, that I have a mother and a daughter, that I had a heart attack, and that *I'm fat.* Isn't that enough for you?"

Ponytail nodded. "Good, we're getting down to hostility. It's much better than ironic disdain." He wrote on a pad. "Here's a refill for your Xarelto and Enalapril."

"Do I have to take these pills forever?" I asked, feeling angry enough to rip the damn prescription to pieces.

Ponytail tapped his pen on his desk, thinking, then said, "When you get down to 210 pounds, I'll reduce the dosage, and we'll see after that."

Yeah right, *when* and not *if*, like he was in control of everything.

He looked at me sideways and said, "Is that enough of an incentive for you to keep coming to our appointments?"

I didn't say goodbye when I left.

§§

We didn't have to call each other to confirm. Ryker, Faith, and I knew where to meet Wednesday morning at 8:00 before work, every Wednesday since 2010, excepting holidays and bad weather days.

This Wednesday, Faith beat me to the Dunkin' Donuts on the northeast corner of Union Square. "You're looking spiffy for a heart-attack patient," she said to me happily when I scooted in beside her at our table.

Without me saying a word, the waitress brought my coffee and two chocolate covered donuts, still hot. When Ryker walked in, Faith had just taken the first bite from her chocolate chip chocolate muffin. That didn't stop her from waving at the waitress to signal for Ryker's bagel with cream cheese.

"You look good," Ryker said to me.

Faith wiped crumbs from her lip and laughed, "That's what I said."

They couldn't get my goat, not when a hot donut was melting in my mouth. I swallowed and said, "You should tell Faith she looks good."

Ryker smiled. "You look great, Faith."

She tittered and answered, "Well, thank you, kind sir. You too."

It never failed. We were in good spirits during breakfast before going together to the Union Square Market.

"What did you think about Callen going rogue last night?" Faith asked.

Sometimes we reviewed TV shows behind the perfume counter in between customers. But it never failed that during Wednesday morning breakfast, Faith talked NCIS Los Angeles.

Ryker didn't answer Faith's burning question. Instead he said, "My mother's arriving from Germany tomorrow. She'll be here for a month."

"Will she stay with you?" Faith asked.

Ryker swallowed a gulp of coffee and nodded Yes.

I shook my head. "Good luck, Ryker. I couldn't stay in the same apartment with my mother for a week. Certainly not a month. I don't know how you're going to do it."

"A hotel for a month would be impossible. Staying with family saves a lot of money," Faith said. She lived with her mother full-time in a multi-family home in Woodhaven. "Your mom will have a wonderful time being with you here. You have an extra bedroom, and Dave likes her, right?"

"They met four years ago when we vacationed in Germany. They got along just fine," he said.

I tried to imagine my mother's reaction if I had a live-in boyfriend. It couldn't be much worse than her reaction to Tanya all those years ago.

"I remember you telling me that you translated everything between Dave and your mother during the entire visit," Faith said.

I snorted, "I'm betting that you 'translated' and omitted anything that one or the other wouldn't like."

Ryker grinned. "I was quite the diplomat. I controlled all the conversation for the two weeks we were there."

"And you'll do the same during this visit, I'm sure," I laughed.

"I haven't decided if I'll bring my mother here with me next Wednesday or if I'll skip our morning outing," Ryker said.

"Oh bring her," Faith insisted, "so I can meet her."

I laughed again. "You won't see me bringing *my* mother here. I keep our weekly excursions to Union Square private, especially from family members."

"Your mother has come to Bergdorf's. I've met her several times, and she's always been nice," Faith said to me.

"You're right," I said with a straight face. "Real nice."

Ryker smirked at my attempt to avoid an ironic tone and said to Faith, "I'll bring my mother to Bergdorf's so you both can meet her. She'll be impressed with the store."

I'd had enough about mothers. I stood up and said, "Let's get to the market."

Outside, we crossed Union Square East and followed Ryker to the maple syrup stand on the left. He'd become a syrup connoisseur over the years and swore that the syrup at the Daniels' stall was twice as good as the syrup at the south end of the square. He bought a jug, then we wandered around tasting samples. Faith laughed at me swooning over a sample of Gouda, until she took a taste and fell in love.

After he tasted some locally-made mustard with a popsicle stick, Ryker took the conversation back a step, "My mother will spend her time in New York comparing German food to what we have here. We'll lose every comparison."

"You don't seem to be bothered by that," I said, sniffing samples of tea leaves.

"No," he smiled. "She's proud of where she lives; that's all."

Faith paid for a loaf of 3-grain bread in the booth next to the cheese and asked, "What do you call your mother? In German, I mean. What's 'mother' in German?"

" 'Mother' is 'Mutter,' but I call her 'Mutti.' It's like saying 'Mama.' "

Faith responded, "My mother is 'Mamu.' It's Polish. She arrived in New York when she was 12, and at home she still speaks Polish." She sighed and went on, "She's almost 80, and it's noticeable that she's deteriorating, especially mentally. I light a candle for her every Sunday."

"It's sad, huh?" Ryker agreed.

"Do you feel like you're stuck taking care of your mother since you live together?" I asked Faith.

Faith shook her head. "Ever since Johnny died, I've lived there for free. I owe her." She shrugged. "And it's not so bad. Someday, I'll be old like that."

I didn't say it out loud, but I hoped I died before I lost my mind. Another heart attack wouldn't be a bad way to go.

A few stands further along, I bought a dozen fresh eggs, and Faith rushed up to me like she was going to slap them out of my hands. I smirked because she did the same bad joke every week. "You know I'll never make you another ham and cheese omelet if you break my eggs."

"Hey, when are you having us over for dinner-time eggs again?" Ryker asked me.

Faith made ummm noises. "Who taught you how to cook, Andy?"

"Not my mother," I snorted. "Cary taught me."

"Your step-father?"

I nodded, without repeating the old story that Cary and Nana had never married. "He's a good guy and is a great cook. Nana can't boil water, but she's funny and talented. Sometimes I hate her."

Faith laughed like I was joking.

"No, really. Everyone loves her *wonderful work*." I dripped the words with fake adoration. "She's impulsive in a way that makes people think she's decisive. I'm the opposite."

"Maybe not so opposite as you think," Ryker said He paid for a jar of local honey, and we kept walking until we got to the fresh poultry stand where I bought a chicken for dinner.

"You know what I think?" Faith said, "I think you're jealous of your mother."

61

I harrumphed. "Me? Jealous of Nana? No."

"Faith's right," Ryker chuckled. "You're jealous."

Together, we studied the fresh shellfish, then moved on.

"Admit it," Faith pushed with a smile. "You're jealous."

"If she weren't so successful," I answered, "she'd be easier to put up with. So yeah, if that makes me jealous, then I'm jealous." I pouted and picked out a lettuce.

Faith put her arm through mine. "I'll share my zucchini with you, if you'd like."

My pique evaporated when she hugged my arm. "Thank you, ma'am," I mimed with a bow.

Ryker looked at his watch. "We'd better head to the bus if we don't want the fragrance manager to get mad that we're late."

"Oh, Ryker, you're the manager," Faith giggled and put her other arm through his, linking us into a threesome.

We made it to Bergdorf's well before the doors opened to the public. I carried our market purchases up to the employee cafeteria and put them in the big fridge, to pick up at closing. Then, as usual, I paid the food service director for the favor with perfume samples.

§§

Wednesday was always a good day for me at Bergdorf's. Thursday and Friday, too. Saturday, you could never tell. It depended on whether it was shopping weather or family weather.

This Saturday was shopping weather, cloudy but no chance of rain.

I waved goodbye to Ms. Randolf-Boche after she helped me meet my week's goal, when I saw Ryker cock his head for me to meet him in the stockroom.

"I didn't want to interrupt you," he said, "but your mother called, maybe 10 minutes ago. She sounded, uh," he paused, "uh, agitated."

"Agitated?" Nana was never agitated. Wound up? Yes. Impatient? Yes. Agitated? No.

"She wants you to call her at home," he told me.

When Nana picked up, she babbled, "Andy, Andy, come over. Come right now." She did indeed sound agitated. Leave it to Ryker to find the right word.

"Nana, what's happened? Are you okay? Is it Cary?"

"I would never have dreamed. And if it weren't for Blue, we wouldn't have known. It seems impossible. Andy, please. Please, Andy, come over."

63

I couldn't remember Nana ever saying "please," and there it was, twice in one conversation. I didn't need anything more. "I'm on my way."

Ryker and Faith waved me off, I caught a taxi, and was at 98th Street and West End Avenue in five minutes. Two police cars and an ambulance were outside Nana's building, and facing the elevator on the 16th floor, my mother was wringing her hands from inside the circle of Cary's arms. Blue paced amid police and emergency personnel in the hallway, as agitated as Nana. The big poodle saw me and galloped over, leaning on me like a… I didn't know like what… like a scared dog.

"What happened?" I asked Cary and Nana, relieved that they were both on their feet and breathing. It was a lot better than I had been imagining.

"Oh, our little neighbor, Amy… Amy …" and my mother lost her voice in a choked-back sob.

Cary took over. "We were reading the *Times* on Nanette's couch when Blue started barking. Barking as if she were terrorized. We didn't understand what set her off, but she pawed at the apartment door wildly."

Nana sniffed and said, "I called her. I told her to lie down and be quiet. She always obeys." She put her fist to her mouth.

"Blue whimpered, then went back to barking. So I opened the door, and she ran to Amy Motheral's apartment next door without letting up on the noise."

"She jumped up on the door, like she does when she wants to open the doorhandle at home," Nana coughed out the words.

Cary took over again, "I rang the doorbell and called out and got no answer."

" 'Try the door,' I told him," Nana moaned.

"The door was locked, but Blue was insistent, so your mother called the police."

"Five minutes. It felt like an hour, but they were here in five minutes," Nana said, pushing her hair out of her face. "Blue was crazy, turning in circles in front of Amy's door and crying."

"After a few tries, the police broke open the door. And there she was on the floor in the bathroom."

"It's only a two-bedroom apartment. It wasn't hard to find her," Nana added.

"We thought she was dead," Cary said. "But the police did CPR and called an ambulance."

"She'd taken pills. Some kind of pills," Nana moaned.

A police officer interrupted the story, "The ambulance is taking your neighbor to New York Presbyterian. Do you know if she has any family?"

Nana shook her head nervously and said, "I've never met her parents. They live somewhere in New Jersey, I think."

"Is Amy going to be okay?" Cary asked.

The officer pursed his lips. "I can't say. But if she makes it, it'll be thanks to you."

Nana burst into tears and blathered, "Thanks to my dog. How could she know? How could a dog be aware of something like that?"

Cary gathered Nana in his arms, and I motioned for him to take her inside his apartment.

"Officer, here's my card," I said. "If there's anything else we can do, or if you get any information, would you let us know?"

He read the card, "Thanks, ah, Mr. Brown. There's one thing. Would you let the Super know that we had to break in. Maybe he can secure the apartment."

I promised I would and watched him get in the elevator with his partner.

In Cary's apartment, Nana was curled up on the living room couch with Blue spread over her lap, like they were holding onto each other. Cary came in, carrying two whiskeys. "Do you want something, Andy?" he asked me.

I shook my head. "You three are heroes," I said. "You may have saved her life."

"I was scared to death when I saw Amy lying there. Oh my god," Nana sniffed and took a swig of whiskey.

Cary collapsed in a chair. "The girl can't be much older than Chloé. What could make her do such a thing? What could be so bad in a young woman's life that she'd want to end it all?"

Nana moaned, "In a building like this, a life like this, we have everything. I don't understand."

I figured people tried to kill themselves every day in New York. In the entire country, probably. Money

66

problems. Love problems. Lost dreams or whatever. I said simply, "We may never know. But she's lucky she lives next to you."

Cary stood up. "I've got to call Chloé, just to make sure she's okay." He got his phone from the table and punched in her code.

While he talked to my daughter, I pushed Blue over and sat down, "I'm glad you called me, Nana. I didn't do anything, but I'm glad you called."

Her bottom lip stuck out and she said in a whine, "You're my baby, Andy. I needed you."

I tipped her head onto my shoulder. "You did great, Nana. You knew to call the police." I patted her knee. "You did great."

§§

"Before you get on the scale," Ponytail said, "why don't you guess your weight for this week."

I smirked. "I didn't lose anything. I ate donuts and drank wine."

"Did you walk?"

"Yes," I groaned. "To and from work, except Wednesday. To and from this damn hospital too. I waste a lot of time going by foot instead of using public transportation."

"Think of it as your contribution to a clean environment," he said, finishing up with the blood pressure machine.

"BP okay?" I asked.

"122/78. Not bad." He stuck the stethoscope on my chest, listened, and made notes on his tablet. "Is your energy level good? Do you get winded when you walk?"

"Why? Is there something wrong. Does my heart sound off somehow?" I felt fear sweep me. It was good that Ponytail had already finished the blood pressure test, because it felt like mine was surging.

"Nothing's wrong. These are normal questions for a post-heart-attack appointment." He paused. "So, Mr., Brown, will you answer me?"

The guy could be a smart aleck. "I'm tired after walking from 69th Street to work on Fifth Avenue, but not breathless. I would've been tired before the stents too, only I never would have thought to walk that far."

He nodded and tapped something onto the tablet again.

"So, let's see if you're right about not losing weight." He pointed me to the scales without getting up.

My jaw dropped. "250," I said. "I don't know how."

"You must have told secrets to someone."

He was holding onto the stupid joke that secrets were the same as pounds. But I thought back through the week. Was it a secret about being jealous of my mother's success? Of her personality and magnetism? Of her life with Cary? Secret or not, it was impossible that me talking about Nana to Ryker and Faith could influence my weight.

As if he read my thoughts, Ponytail said, "Changing habitual thought and activity patterns can influence metabolism more effectively than dieting. And as you know, metabolism controls how a person burns calories. Or maybe you were stressed this week and burned calories. It's not an experiment I'm conducting. I just want results for you."

I looked at him sideways.

"Yes," he reiterated, "I want you to be healthy."

I took a deep breath. He still seemed like a self-important hospital lacky to me. "Is that all for today?"

He stood up and walked me to the office door. "Next week, same time, same place."

I wondered if he knew he sounded like an announcer for the old Batman T.V. series: "Same bat station…."

I walked through the door and literally ran into Chloé coming toward the door, knocking her glasses off-center.

I stepped back in surprise. "What are you doing here?" Suddenly suspicious, I asked, "Are you checking up on me?"

My daughter's laughter jingled through the hospital hallway. "No. But I knew where you'd be. I have some good news I wanted to share." She was beaming.

I noticed that Ponytail was still standing in the doorway waiting for me to leave. "Ah…," I stumbled, trying to remember Ponytail's name, and finally skipped over it, saying, "…ah, do you remember my daughter from my hospital visit?" I didn't have any problem with Chloé's name: "Chloé Brown," I said as a reintroduction.

Luckily Ponytail took over and said his own name: "Yes. I'm Bradley Matthews, your father's cardiac nurse practitioner."

Chloé put out her hand to shake. "I remember you, Mr. Matthews."

"Please, call me Brad. Everyone does."

Everyone except me, I thought.

"Daddy is stable now, right?" she asked.

Ponytail nodded. "He's responding well after the intervention."

"I didn't mean to interrupt your session. I just wanted to tell Daddy something." Her eyes were twinkling, and I could tell she was going to bubble over. "I just got word that an article of mine was accepted by *JAMA Dermatology*. Yea!" She applauded herself.

"That's great, Chloé. I knew it'd happen," I told her, patting her on the back.

"*The Journal of the American Medical Association*?" Ponytail asked. "Your father told me you were a …. " He turned to me with a question in his eyes.

My chest puffed out. "She's a physical therapist, but she's always discovering something. This time, she found a way to stop eczema."

Chloé blushed, almost as red as her glasses. "Daddy's exaggerating. But yes, I had a PT patient with a crushed elbow. Before, she'd had eczema like you wouldn't believe, all her life, up and down her arms. But when pins were put in her elbow, within a couple of weeks, the eczema disappeared. I did a study on the positive effects of titanium with 4500 orthopedic implant patients suffering with skin disease in New York and New Jersey, and…," she did a jig in the hallway making her spiky hair vibrate, "…yes, my results are going to be published."

"It's not her first published article," I said proudly. I should have stopped there, but I pushed on with the intention of putting Ponytail in his place. "Do you publish in medical journals?"

To my disappointment, Ponytail nodded and said, "Sometimes." He turned to Chloé and said, "I'd love to

71

read your findings. Let me know when it comes out." He took a card from his wallet and gave it her. "Please."

Chloé did a mini-curtsy, "It will be my pleasure." I knew she was telling the truth. She was thrilled to share her work with anyone who was interested.

An old lady in an ugly navy coat walked up to us.

"Ah, Ms. Campbell, come in," Ponytail said, ushering the woman into his office. "See you next week, Mr. Brown."

"Isn't it great, Daddy?" Chloé crooned.

Absolutely great. My daughter was the smartest girl in the world, as far as I could tell. She'd ace an IQ test. I couldn't imagine where she got her ideas or her motivation. No one told her to research titanium, or any of the other bizarre subjects she wrote about in her spare time.

"Are you celebrating the publication with George tonight?" I asked.

"He's taking me to Luke's Lobster for dinner, but I need to celebrate now, before I go to the Hanger Clinic. Let's go for a coffee together! Please!"

"Yes, of course."

She wagged like a happy dog, and we headed to the elevator.

From the sidewalk, I called Ryker to tell him I'd be late. That was one of the perks of being the best and oldest salesperson in the department: When I needed a few extra minutes here and there, I took them.

§§

My daughter's boyfriend stood on the sidewalk where the sinking sun projected light through the leaves. "Hi, George." I put out my hand to shake. "Chloé invited me over to help you climb the stairs to her apartment."

He opened the front door without laughing at my delightful joke and let me pass into the building.

"She's upstairs," he said.

I didn't visit my daughter often at her home because of the 45 steps leading to her 3rd floor apartment. I girded myself for the marathon climb and followed George up. If I wanted to test my stents, this would do it.

Nana and Cary were sitting on Chloé's couch drinking white wine, and my daughter came in from the kitchen with a glass for me. "Thanks for coming, Daddy. You're not huffing and puffing!" she noted happily.

"You can blame the damn nurse for that. He forces me to exercise."

"What *is* the difference between a nurse and a nurse practitioner?" Nana asked.

Cary replied, "A better question is, what's the difference between a doctor and a nurse practitioner? They both write prescriptions."

"Ask that nurse of yours to explain the difference next time you visit him," Nana said.

Chloé pulled a chair up next to mine and said to George, "Sit over there, babe, next to Cary." She smiled, but it wasn't her jolly smile. It was an imitation of a smile I'd never seen on her face before.

She took a breath and said, "I wanted to tell you all at once."

Oh no, I thought. She's moving to Africa or dying of cancer. I tried not to listen.

Then she said it. "I'm pregnant."

Five people in the apartment were totally silent, even my mother.

Then George chuckled. "You're joking," he said in a light-hearted voice. "You scared me for a minute. Funny girl."

I watched Chloé take a breath. Still no smile. "No. No joke here. The home pregnancy test showed positive this afternoon, and I've been feeling nauseous for a while."

Nana was the one to change the mood: "That's wonderful, sweetheart." She didn't wrap the words in enthusiasm, but she said what had to be said. She stood up and tugged on Cary's hand, "But we should leave you and George alone to discuss this… blessed event."

No one was more an atheist than my mother. The phrase "blessed event" coming out of her mouth was like asphalt melting under your feet on a hot day.

George's mouth hung open. Clearly, he wasn't sure if he wanted to believe what he'd heard. "When? When did you find out? When did it happen? How?"

"Don't leave, Nana. I want you all here," Chloé said. "I need to decide what to do, and I need all of you to help me." Her voice was trembling. She turned to George to answer. "When? Maybe one of those times we didn't use a condom, or maybe it just happened? They're not 100% effective, you know."

I heard a trace of resentment in her voice, though it was well covered by her general good nature. But me, I glared at George and barked, "Sometimes you don't use a condom? What are you, 12 years old?" I grumbled under my breath, "How incredibly stupid."

Suddenly I was sorry to have blurted out my feelings in front of Chloé. I backpedaled with, "We'll all be there for you, Chloé. I promise. I'll be your #1 babysitter."

Her expression softened. "Thanks, Daddy. But…." Her voice drifted off.

Nana stepped in again and took charge. "Yes, before you bother making choices or changes, first we have to get you to a doctor."

"What choices and changes?" I said. "Of course, everything will change."

George's tone continued light when he finally spoke. "She's right. It was just one of those over-the-counter tests. You haven't seen a doctor." It was like he was reviewing the facts, trying to compute the details in a frozen mind. "You need to see a real doctor." He shifted his eyes to Nanette, then back to Chloé. "You'll arrange a doctor's appointment, right?"

Couldn't the jerk at least tell Chloé he loved her. She was going to have his baby. He should be cuddling her. I felt a growl rising in my throat, and I gave the son of a bitch an evil stare.

The stare must have worked because finally he said, "You know I love you, babe. We'll handle everything, you and me, and your family. You're not alone."

Chloé couldn't help herself. The tears were welling up, and her voice cracked. "I'm just a little scared is all."

Cary spoke up, "Of course, you're scared. Being pregnant is a big deal."

I almost laughed at him saying the American expression "big deal" in his French accent, but I kept focused and serious.

"Can I come to your place tomorrow morning to make a gyno appointment?" she asked Nana.

"Absolutely. George is right: don't do anything alone. Come for breakfast."

My daughter choked back tears at her grandmother's words. Me too, for that matter. My ex, Tanya, was a million miles away in California and wouldn't be any help. Nana and me, we were the ones who had pulled Chloé through her teenage years. I had bought Tampax and sat with her while she researched contraceptives. Nana had listened instead of lectured about boys.

Nana went on, "If you have this baby, it'll be the most beautiful baby in the world," and Chloé's tears began.

If? Why wouldn't she have the baby? What was Nana talking about?

"You're probably full of hormones," George said. "You'll be crying all the time. *If* you're pregnant, that is. We don't really know yet."

Chloé breathed deeply and seemed to calm down. She swept her eyes over our faces. "So, that's my news. Would you mind now if I had some private time?"

"You want me to go too?" George asked.

She gave a faint smile and nodded. "I'm really tired."

We filed out, giving her hugs and kisses. As we herded down the steps, she called out to us in a stage whisper, "Don't tell anyone about this, okay?"

Back home, my mind was crowded with images of stumbling through the first months of parenting a baby daughter with Tanya. Memories and regrets kept me awake until dawn.

§§

"Of course, I'm staying," I told Chloé at 8:30 Thursday morning in the waiting room at Weill Cornell Clinic on 72nd Street. "I was at the cheerleading try-outs for high school. I'm going to be at the baby try-outs too." Truthfully, I was edgy about being with my daughter during a gynecological exam, but hey, this was the biggest moment of her life so far, and I was going to be there to support her.

Chloé's support team included me and Nana. George was at some kind of on-line business interview, and Cary had an early morning rendezvous at PNB Bank.

Nana held Chloé's hand and asked, "Do you like this doctor? Because if not, I can get you into my ob/gyn."

Chloé was too distracted to answer. If it had been me, I've have replied that no one liked a gynecologist or a urologist. But I kept quiet.

The receptionist led us to Dr. Perkins' office. Instead of asking about Chloé's entourage, the doctor started with, "You're looking healthy, Ms. Brown. Tell me what brings you in today."

Nana and I both stayed quiet. That was one for the record books.

Chloé answered, "I think I'm pregnant."

Then the questions began. "You've taken an over-the-counter test?" the doctor asked.

She nodded and simply said, "Positive."

"Last period?"

"Six weeks ago."

"How many sexual partners?"

"One."

"Does he know about the positive test?"

Chloé smiled and answered, "Yes. We've been partners for a while.

"Have you been trying to get pregnant?"

Her eyes popped wide open, and I swear she giggled. "No!" she said.

"Unprotected sex?"

"Yes," she said

The image of George without a condom made a growl rise in my throat. Chloé must have heard it, because for the first time during the morning, she smirked, and changed her answer, "Sometimes."

"Do you use a contraceptive?"

"No."

The doctor nodded and pushed a button on his phone. A nurse appeared, and Perkins said, "Ms. Delany will take you for blood and urine samples. She'll take your blood pressure too." His gaze played over me and Nana, before returning to Chloé. "Your delegation can go with you or stay in the waiting area, as you wish."

We didn't give her a chance to answer. We followed her down the hallway. But when the doc took Chloé into the exam room, I waited outside while my mother went in. I'd gone through the exams with Tanya when she was pregnant 26 years ago, and that was enough for a lifetime.

§§

A half hour later, I was escorted back to the doctor's office to join Nana and Chloé.

Perkins addressed Chloé, "You are pregnant, Ms. Brown, due in approximately 7½ months."

I saw Chloé's face go white. She looked at me, then at her grandmother. "So we're within the timeframe for…" She seemed to lose her train of thought.

The doctor finished her sentence, "… for terminating the pregnancy? Yes, easily. You have time to think about it."

"What's to think about?" I said. "Everything is in order, right, Doc?"

Before the doctor could answer, Nana said, "This is Chloé's story, Andy. The next chapter is hers. Not yours."

"What do you mean?" I said, feeling dense.

It was the doctor who answered. "Your daughter has decisions to make now that she knows her situation."

I looked at Chloé, but it was Nana who spoke. "Andy, he means that she can choose to have the baby or not."

"And there's adoption. That's an alternate choice," Chloé added.

"But you know the father. He's moving in with you soon. We're all here for you." I didn't understand what else there was to consider.

Dr. Perkins spoke to Chloé, "The receptionist will make a follow-up appointment for a month from now. If you have questions or concerns or want to see us sooner for any reason at all, just call." He stood up and reached out to shake her hand.

Outside on the sidewalk, I said, "You can't have an abortion, Chloé. That's what you were talking about, wasn't it?"

"It's none of our business, Andy," Nana jumped in firmly.

"What's with you, Nana? You always have an opinion about what other people should do. And this is your granddaughter, so of course, it's your business."

Chloé put her hand on my arm. "I'm not sure what I want to do, Daddy. I might not be ready for parenthood."

I laughed. "Believe me, no one is ever ready for a baby, no matter what they say."

She smiled softly at me with an "I love you" expression in her eyes. Or maybe it was a "You're so stupid" expression. Anyhow, she said, "I just need to think about it."

I opened my mouth to reply, but Nana took me by the elbow and squeezed hard enough that I yelped.

"Are you walking to work, Daddy?" Chloé asked.

Ah, she'd accompany me on the walk so we could talk, and she'd tell me she'd name the baby after me.

When I nodded, she kissed my cheek and said, "Bye. I'll stay in touch."

My vision of a baby named Andy dissolved.

Chloé turned to Nana to say, "I'm heading west. You want to come?"

And they were gone.

§§

"I couldn't believe it," I told Faith.

Ryker nodded, "In this day and age advanced medical and techno information, how can an adult get pregnant by surprise?"

Faith laughed out loud. "Ryker. It's sex. We don't think about it, no matter what age we are. We just do it."

The opening bell hadn't rung yet. The three of us were sitting on stools stocking and arranging the lower counters.

"She'll have the baby," I said.

"Well, sure," Faith said. "It's not like she's a homeless high school student who doesn't know which of her six boyfriends is the father. It's Chloé."

"I'm going home and checking my condom stash," Ryker said.

Faith giggled, "You don't need condoms to keep from getting pregnant."

"But I need condoms," he replied, winking at her.

"I don't have a condom stash," I said.

Faith's jaw dropped open. "Andy, even I have a condom stash. What's wrong with you?"

I reached for another box of Joe Malone's Lime Basil & Mandarin to unpack. "Come on. I'm middle-aged, divorced, I can't ride a bike, and I look ridiculous when I swim with my white stomach and legs flopping around.

Can you imagine someone wanting to see me naked in bed?"

"It doesn't have to be in bed," Ryker quipped.

Faith leaned toward me to ask, "So it's been a long time?"

"Faith, we're not going to have this discussion," I said, putting Peony & Blush on the shelf.

She grinned at me. "I'll tell you my last time if you tell me yours."

"No."

"Oh come on. I live with my mother. You're bound to have bedded down with someone more recently than me.

Ryker shook his head, "Am I the only one here with private parts that work." Quickly, he held up his hand in a stop signal. "Don't answer that. For me, three times this week already."

"Ahhhh," I groaned. "That's no fair. You live with Dave."

"So? You used to have a wife. How long ago was that?"

I did the subtraction. On her last birthday, Chloé turned 26. She'd been 15 when Tanya left, and the marriage had been sexless for at least a year before that. Oh my god, regular sex was 13 years ago.

"My ex has nothing to do with my current status," I insisted. "It's just that I have a busy life."

"Okay, here's my life on a platter for you guys to judge," Faith said. "I went out four times with Leonard Penis last month."

"Leonard Penis?" Ryker gawked.

Faith turned coyly to the side. "It's just a nickname," she chuckled.

"Did you take him to your mother's house?" I asked trying to keep my face straight.

"We went to his apartment," Faith said. "But Mamu wouldn't have minded if I'd brought him home. She's so hard of hearing she wouldn't have realized what was going on."

"It's your turn, Andy. Tell us," Ryker pushed.

I sidestepped, "It's embarrassing."

"Six months," Ryker guessed.

I pointed upwards.

"A year," Faith said.

I pointed up again.

The opening bell rang.

"Tell us!" Faith demanded. "Customers will be here any minute."

I put my hands on the counter edge to pull myself up, but my shoulders slumped in shame. "I took a woman to Chloé's graduation party when she got her master's degree, we had a few drinks, and … you know. That was four years ago."

"*Four years ago!*" Ryker and Faith shrieked, choking back laughter. Their hysteria was the reason I never told anybody details about my private life.

"Ah, Ms. Taylor, what a pleasure to see you today," I said, turning my back on my colleagues to pull in my first client of the day. When I glanced behind me, they were still sniggering in my honor. If I could have, without Ms.

Taylor seeing me, I would have shot them the bird. Or just shot them dead.

§§

"So what's a nurse practitioner, exactly?" I asked.

Ponytail put his finger to his lips to shush me and continued listening through the stethoscope. He instructed me to take deep breaths, listened, tapped my back, and listened. He led me to the cursed scales, and typed his damn notes.

"What were you saying, Mr. Brown?"

"You're a nurse practitioner. What's the difference between you and a nurse?"

He looked at his watch and sat down. "I'm halfway between a doctor and a nurse," he said. "NP's have bachelor and master's degrees, and then, for my cardiac specialty, a student takes 700 hours of clinical hours before sitting for the certification exam and applying for extra licensing."

I didn't want to look impressed, so I murmured, "Oh," and looked over his shoulder. "That was enough for you, without going the whole way to becoming a doctor."

He smirked as if my barb had missed its mark. "Like a doctor, NP's can have private offices, prescribe treatments, order tests, and diagnose patients," he told me. "Me, I prefer people more than technique. I like dealing with heart patients more than heart surgery."

I kept quiet.

"I take it that you're feeling okay. No palpitations, no shortness of breath?"

I shook my head.

"Your weight today is 244 pounds. What do you think of that?"

I felt the words on my tongue: "I think you're a smug egotistical nurse practitioner." Instead of saying that, I stood up to leave.

Ponytail rubbed his chin and asked rather loudly, "How many pounds is it that you've lost since the stent intervention?"

I could do the stupid math, even if I didn't have a stupid master's degree. I'd lost 24 pounds, and I left without saying goodbye.

§§

My ringing cell phone distracted me from scrolling through the T.V. program list for the night, but I answered. If I'd glanced at the caller ID, I would have skipped the call.

As my ex-wife talked, I stretched out and let the soft yellow leather on the arm of the couch cradle my head.

Tanya was in the middle of saying something: "It was only a couple of weeks ago that we talked. She said he was moving in with her." Ah, she was giving me a run-down about George. "I gave her my opinion…," she said, not surprising me at all, "… that it was a great idea. They'll save money; they'll learn to relax totally around each other; they'll learn to be a committed couple."

I couldn't stop myself from saying, "Yes, just like you and your committed boyfriends."

I listened to the laughter of my ex-wife on the phone speaker. It was like glass breaking into tiny pieces and falling from the sky, unfortunately similar to Chloé's tinkling laugh.

I got up to search the fridge for something to eat and kept listening.

"Now Andy, don't let jealousy make you cynical. I've been with Hal for almost two years. We have a wonderful relationship."

Hal Johnson: I'd looked him up on the internet. Late 60's, rich Hollywood producer, three former wives, glass house on the beach. "He'll never marry you, Tanya."

"I don't want to be married again, Andy. You were wonderful, but you were enough. I have a good salary from Matthew and a large allowance from Hal, and I am perfectly happy." There was the glass laugh again. "That's what I want for our baby girl too, for her to be perfectly happy."

When she'd moved to L.A. leaving me and Chloé high and dry eleven years ago, Tanya had found a job as a make-up artist for Matthew McConaughey. I imagined various scenarios for how she achieved this feat, but I never asked.

I pulled out two Chinese food cartons left-over from Tuesday night. "And did she tell you she's pregnant?"

There was silence on the other end of the line. Blessed silence, weird and surprising silence from my ex. How wonderful to be able to shut her up for a few seconds.

"Pregnant?" she whispered.

"Yes. A doctor confirmed it a few days back."

I waited, pleased that my daughter had confided in me and not Tanya. I dumped General Tso chicken and broccoli fried rice on a plate and put it in the microwave.

Finally, Tanya said, "Okay then. If Matthew doesn't mind, I'll change my airline reservation. I was coming at the end of the month, but now I'll come right before her due date. When is that?"

"The doctor said 7½ months or so."

"I'm sure George is thrilled," she said.

I kept silent.

"So don't give me details, you Scrooge. I'll call our girl and get the good stuff from her."

I closed my eyes.

"How is Nanette doing?" Tanya asked lightly. "And Cary?"

"They're the same as ever," I answered.

"What bliss. Always the lovebirds, no matter what their age," she responded. "Prepare yourself, Andy. When I come to New York, I'll want to stay in your apartment. It's so much more charming than a hotel room."

So much cheaper, is what she meant. I decided not to worry about it. I had months to devise a way to avoid my ex-wife no matter where she stayed.

The microwave dinged. I took out the plate and sat down at the table with soy sauce and a half-full bottle of Pinot Noir.

When Tanya finally finished the conversation, I switched on the Cloudbox and finished my dinner with Keith Jarrett's piano and *Bye Bye Blackbird.* It was so much better than the sound of Tanya's voice.

I was rinsing my plate to put in the dishwasher when the phone rang again. "Shit," I said out loud. "What did she forget?"

But it was an unidentified caller. I dried my hands and answered.

"Hi. This is Ned Lewis. I met you through Carl at the airshow party a few weeks back."

"Oh yes. Hello, Ned."

"If you remember, I promised you tickets to City Ballet. I hope you're still interested; I have three tickets available, center orchestra, row L, for Saturday night."

I paused. Three tickets. That was an odd number.

Ned went on, "They're free, of course. My gift. I can leave them at the Will-Call window."

I shifted into grateful-recipient gear and responded, "Ned, that's very kind of you. I accept, with pleasure."

I heard the young man relax, like he'd been anxious to talk to a stranger. That trait would make fundraising difficult, I thought.

"There are three pieces on the program: Robbins, Martins, and a new choreographer, Jamar Roberts," Ned said.

I knew the name Robbins because of West Side Story. The others meant nothing to me. "I'm looking forward to it. This Saturday, right?"

"And come to the stage entrance after the show. I'll give you a backstage tour."

"Is that so you can be sure I don't give the tickets away to Bergdorf clients?"

He chuckled. "Oh, I'm embarrassed. I hoped you'd forgotten I said that."

"Just joking," I laughed. "My mother will be jealous of a tour."

I heard a tense intake of breath on the line, "Cary said they had a subscription. I can do the same for them when they come." I bet he got tired trying to please everybody who could be a potential donor.

"I'll tell them, Ned. And I'll see you at the stage door Saturday night."

§§

Back on the couch, I muted *Seinfeld* during the commercial and dialed Nana. When she answered. "Do you happen to be going to the ballet this Saturday night?" I asked.

"I'll call you back. We're eating dinner."

"Two minutes, that's all. Tell Cary to keep chewing."

"No," she said. I wasn't sure if she meant about Cary chewing or the ballet. Then she went on, "Our tickets are for… , I don't know… they're for later. A couple of weeks from now."

"That's all I wanted to know," I said. "Goodnight."

"No, wait. You can't hang up on that note. Why do you want to know?"

"Cary's friend at New York City Ballet just offered me tickets for Saturday night. I was wondering if you'd be there."

I heard a muffled conversation. She was no doubt telling Cary about the tickets.

"Take Chloé. I'm sure she'd love to go," Nana said.

"I've got three tickets."

"Well, there you go. It's perfect for you, Chloé, and George."

An evening with George wasn't my ideal Saturday night, but I couldn't see a way out of it if I asked Chloé – unless I sold the third ticket.

I changed the subject: "By the way, your neighbor, the suicide, I never heard the end of the story."

"I bet you're watching T.V. and you're talking because it's a long commercial break."

How did she know such a thing?

"Amy moved back in with her parents in Jersey City," Nana said, answering my question. "I hear that she's taking medication for depression." Without taking a breath, she went on, "Back to the ballet, your tickets are for the Martins-Robbins-Roberts performance?"

I wasn't sure, but she took my silence as Yes.

"You'll like the show," Nana continued. "Everyone loves *Glass Pieces*, the *Black Swan Pas de Deux* is a modern classic, and the buzz about *Emanon* is good."

"Wayne Shorter's *Emanon*?"

"I think so. The NYCB choreographer -- Roberts, I think his name is – he's in residence from Alvin Ailey's Dance Theater, so he'd know that kind of composer. Look it up on the web site," she said.

If there was music from my saxophone hero, maybe I'd enjoy a night at the ballet. "How do you know all these details, Nana?" I didn't add that it was unnatural for an old person like her to have a good memory. "I'll have to write everything on my wrist to remember all the names, like I used to do for college exams."

"Everything will be in the ballet's program, Andy."
I interpreted that to mean, *Don't be stupid, Andy.* There
was a split second pause, and she went on, "You cheated
on tests to get through college? You're a cheater?"

"It was a million years ago, Nana. Forget I said
anything."

"But we paid for your education, and you missed
out on…."

I held the phone away from my ear. "Goodnight,
Nana. Enjoy dinner," I said from a distance and hung up.

Advertisements were still rolling across the
television screen.

§§

I sent Chloé a text: "If you're still awake, call me. Good news."

The phone rang immediately.

"Hi Daddy," her tinkling voice came through loud and clear.

"What are you doing at 11:00 at night?"

"I could ask you the same thing," she laughed.

"Me, I'm picking out my clothes for tomorrow morning."

"You still do that?"

"Of course. It helps me slide into the morning with no stress. Now, your turn. Tell me."

"I'm reading the *Times* in bed, next to George who is watching *Ghostbusters* for the 100th time."

I wished I hadn't asked what she was doing. Too late. "Turn to the Arts section."

Without a question, she obeyed. I heard the pages rattle.

"Okay, what am I looking for?" she asked.

"Search around for New York City Ballet."

"Oh, big article, two photos."

An image of Chloé snuggling next to George tried to worm its way into my mind, but I refused its entrance. I didn't want to think about what they were wearing. Me, I wore cotton pajama shorts that showed off my knobby knees and a matching shirt.

"Do you remember Ned…, ah, Ned somebody, at the air show, a gym friend of Cary's?"

"Sure. Ned Lewis."

"He gave me three tickets for the ballet on Saturday night. Something about Swan Lake and jazz by Wayne Shorter. Do you and George want to join me?"

There were two-voice murmurs, and Chloé came back and said, "That'd be great. We both have too much work to join you for dinner before the show. Can we just meet you at the Koch Theater?"

"7:45?"

"See you there," she said. "And Daddy, sweet dreams."

"You too, sweetheart." Then a light went off in my head. "I forgot, one other thing."

I paused to make sure she hadn't hung up, then went on. "I talked to your mother today. She said she was going to wait to come to New York until closer to your due date."

I didn't get a response and looked at the phone to make sure we were still connected. "Chloé?"

"You told her?" The sparkle in her voice changed to something like cracked ice.

"Well, sure. She didn't want to come twice, for George's moving in and for the baby." I sneered when I added, "She wanted to stay at my apartment. Ha! Just like her, always taking advantage."

99

"One thing, Daddy. One thing I asked, and you don't respect me enough to do the *one* thing I asked of you."

"What? What are you talking about? Chloé?"

I heard her breath coming fast like she was out of bed and pacing wildly around the apartment. "I told you not to tell anyone I was pregnant."

"Sweetie, come on. Don't be like that. I was surprised you hadn't already told Tanya. She's your mother."

I heard a muffled scream as if she were holding the phone against her stomach.

Then she spoke again, but low, growling, like I'd never heard before, a million miles away from her normal cheery lighthearted tone. "Yes. She's my mother." She was silent.

I kept silent too, because I knew better than anyone that it was poison for Tanya to know too much, for her to think that your story was the same as her story and she could do with it as she pleased.

"Ah, Chloé, ah, I'm sorry," I said quietly. "I didn't think."

"Obviously," she spit.

I tried to backpedal with, "But you would've told her at some point. It's earlier than you wanted, and I'm sorry, but finally, it'll be okay."

She hissed, "You are so stupid," and I heard the line go dead.

I sat on the edge of the bed and stared at the phone. I thought back to Tanya's pregnancy. She had been on hormone overload, with mood swings like a hurricane, screaming, laughing, crying, starving, exhausted. My daughter had entered that crazy world apparently, wildly over-reacting to my slip of the tongue.

It was a good thing I hadn't told her about Ryker and Faith's response to her news when I told them. To be truthful, I'd forgotten that she wanted me to keep the pregnancy a secret. Maybe Ponytail was right, and secrets could make a person crazy, at least a person like my daughter.

§§

Ponytail watched the digital screen as the blood pressure sleeve tightened around my arm. "By the way," he said, "your daughter sent me an advance proof copy of her article in JAMA."

"I haven't seen it yet. I saw the one published last year about left-handed and right-handed teeth brushing. One of her patients had a mangled right hand from a factory accident. While they were doing repetitive exercises to rebuild his motion, he told Chloé he had a dental checkup coming up. She made some chit chat about her own teeth and cavities, and anyhow, it came out that his cavities were on the right side. Hers too. And they were both right-handed."

Ponytail entered my BP numbers on his tablet. "I'm going to take a blood sample today," he said and took out a syringe.

While he stuck me, I looked the other way and kept talking. "Chloé did research in five states, New York, Massachusetts, New Hampshire, Vermont, and Connecticut, I think it was, finding dental statistics for the last ten years that backed up her guess that right-handed people brushed the left teeth more naturally and more thoroughly. She published an article in the American Journal of Dentistry about educating patients in bi-lateral brushing to compensate for being right- or left-handed."

He put the stethoscope to my chest, and I chuckled, "Who would have come up with such a kooky idea except my daughter?"

"I need you to be quiet, Mr. Brown."

We were both silent while he listened, front and back. He took my pulse.

"Have you been short of breath?"

I shook my head No.

"Have you had any unusual stress this week?"

Tanya's call and Chloé's bizarre anger came to mind. I answered, "Nothing out of the ordinary."

"You're blood pressure is up, Mr. Brown: 139/82. Let's check your weight." I did my regular pose on the scale. Ponytail nodded and announced, "238 pounds," as if I couldn't see the digital screen.

He sat behind his desk, tapped in notes, and said, "Since everything else is in order, I want you to stop taking your Enalapril for a week, and instead, ingest more potassium. We'll see if that brings your BP down."

I had no idea how to ingest potassium. In fact, I wasn't sure what potassium was, other than a fertilizer for rose bushes.

He looked up from his tablet and seemed to be waiting for me to say something. Finally, he repeated, "Potassium."

I had nothing to say.

"Do you know what to eat to get potassium?"

He was crazy if he thought I was going to admit to being stupid.

He went on, "Salad, tomatoes, potatoes."

I huffed. I ate those things without some high and mighty nurse practitioner telling me.

"Also, bananas, avocados, apricots, and peanut butter."

I nodded. I hadn't had a good peanut butter sandwich in a long time. Maybe a peanut butter/banana sandwich with apricot jam. My stomach growled.

Ponytail smirked at the sound, then dropped his face back to neutral. "Try a banana a day."

I gave him a salute. "Is that all for today?"

He stood up. "Please thank your daughter for sending me the *JAMA Dermatology* article. She's a good researcher." He cocked his head to the side and added, "And a good writer."

He should tell her himself -- that's what I thought, but after the fit Chloé threw about me divulging "her story" to her mother, I smiled and left without a word.

§§

I wouldn't say it was a habit, but I was used to leaving my building in the morning, passing the bus stop, and walking toward Columbus Circle. Except today, ugh, it was raining. Not a downpour, but enough to be messy. I went back up to my apartment and changed into my waterproof Moncler boots and slipped into my Burberry. Last year, the raincoat had been on 75% sale, plus my discount.

A bag with my Bruno Magli's in one hand and my giant umbrella in the other, I tried to be upbeat about walking in the rain. I was only half successful. At Bergdorf's, I went directly to the men's employee locker room and peeled off the soggy coat and boots. It took me 10 minutes to rearrange my hair, and then I changed out of my damp-ish shirt into my just-in-case shirt hanging in my locker.

I looked in the wall mirror and judged the result: not bad. But… I squinted at my image. Yes, my clothes were too big. The shirt bunched into my belt that I had cinched to hold up my slacks. That was not the way slacks were meant to stay up.

I looked at my watch. Only 10:20. I dashed to the elevator and went to the top floor.

"Dominic!" I called across Bergdorf's behind-the-scenes area full of ironing boards, sewing machines, steam machines, rolling clothing racks, and workers handling clothes that would soon be on the sales floors.

A short man, with a measuring tape looped around his neck, waved and started coming toward me. Short was not an exaggeration. Dominic was 5'2" with lifts in his shoes.

"Andy, what a pleasure," Dominic said, reaching for my hand with both of his. "What brings you up here to the nerve-center of the building?"

I did a 360° turn for him and said, "Look at me. My clothes look as if they belong to a giant. What can you do for me?" Dominic Berlini was not just the best tailor at Bergdorf's. As far as I was concerned, he was the best in NYC.

He pursed his lips, circled me, and shook his head. "You've lost weight," he announced and leaned in close to whisper, "Are you sick?"

I growled and answered, "I had a heart attack, and they put me on a diet." That wasn't technically true, but it was easier than explaining about the damned nurse practitioner.

Dominic pulled his chin in like a turtle. "Oh yes, I heard about the drama you pulled down in Fragrance, being shipped out in an ambulance. Well, you look terrible. I can't believe your clients haven't told you."

"You're such a sweetie," I said with as much sarcasm as I could muster. "Can you fix my clothes?" I repeated.

He circled me again and frowned. "Come in Tuesday morning at 9:00 with as many of your clothes as you can carry. I'll take measurements and see what I can save. But I think you're going to have to go on a shopping spree for yourself."

On my way to the Fragrance Department, I passed by the jewelry counter on the main floor to sneak a peek at the gold Son of Poseidon signet ring. Ten minutes later, my mood and confidence were soaring when I greeted my first customer at the perfume counter.

It took me a half-hour to log a $426 sale in my pocket notepad, and I warmed up a smile for my next client. By lunch, I'd tallied $1188 in sales, a bit on the low side for me, but with a lot of time left in the day.

I called Chloé and left a message, "With the rain, let's meet a little early tonight. 7:40? Is that good? Inside the lobby."

§§

During my afternoon break, I saw Chloé had called and listened to her message, "Daddy, I'm not going tonight. I'm still furious about you telling Mom what was supposed to be my secret, and I'd seethe all through the ballet." My stomach rolled over. Wow, she was really upset. I'd never seen her hold onto a grudge, at least not toward me. Could I have been wrong about this reaction being a hormone spike?

I called her back immediately. Without a greeting, I launched in, "Chloé, you take the tickets. You and George go to the ballet. Consider it my apology gift for upsetting you." What had I done that was so horrible? "Take a friend with you for the third ticket." I flashed back to the conversation I'd had with my ex. "I said more than I should have to your mother," I admitted, "and I …."

Chloé interrupted me so loudly that I had to hold the phone away from my ear: "It's MY life and MY decision to do what I want and to tell who I want. NOT YOURS."

Well, I got it. I had crossed my daughter's Rubicon. "Chloé, I understand."

"Mom called me, of course. She had to have all the details." Chloé slipped into an imitation of her mother's high pitched voice, "Who? When? How? What? Who?

When? How? What?" She groaned and went on, "All I could do was keep repeating that I didn't know yet."

I imagined the conversation with Tanya and echoed the groan. "I overstepped. I am sorry for 'telling your story,' as Nana would say."

I broke off for a split second with the horrible thought that Chloé had described our fight to her grandmother. "Nana doesn't know, does she? I promise I won't do such a thing again. No need to make this a family crisis."

"Of course, I told Nana. We both decided to never trust you again."

I knew this song and dance. When my mother and my daughter colluded melodramatically, it was a sign that the disagreement had turned into entertainment.

"The least I can do to make up for my blunder is give you the three tickets. Enjoy the show on your own. But Ned Lewis is expecting us at the stage door after the performance, so you have to go there to explain."

"Ned Lewis, the guy from the Air Show?"

"He thinks he's going to give us a backstage tour. You'll recognize him. Tell him whatever you want, but I don't want him to be standing there all night without anyone showing up."

After a silent pause, there was a big huff of air from Chloé's side of the conversation. Then, "Oh Daddy. I was so mad at you. So mad!"

I nodded and didn't reply.

"You'll listen next time I ask you to do something?"

I nodded and said somberly, "From now on, always, I promise."

She grunted, "You're exaggerating."

"Not by much," I said, knowing that my smile was coming through the phone. It wasn't a mocking smile, just a loving dad smile.

After a giant sigh, Chloé said, "Okay. Let's have a cultural night together."

"Do I have to be nice to George?"

That earned me a laugh.

"7:40, in the lobby," I said and signed off.

§§

At George's suggestion, we checked our coats and umbrellas instead of dripping them through the aisle and over the knees of people in the audience. The seats were great, in the center of the orchestra level, far enough back that we could see the stage floor.

With the orchestra playing, the curtain went up. Dancers in colored leotards randomly crossed the stage. Three dancing couples wandered in, and the walkers switched their style. Rhythm and style shifts happened again and again.

Then the music changed, and a procession of Egyptian silhouettes passed along the back of the stage. A pair of dancers took center stage and did a seductive hieroglyphic ballet.

The third section of music had dancers moving in groups, with more and more dancers entering, following the abstract music.

At the first intermission, I turned to Chloé next to me and said, "They didn't look like dancers at all, but it was a dance, a beautiful dance."

She nodded. "That means you liked it?"

From Chloé's other side, George said, "I expected tutus, and I got a city scene. And the music didn't have a melody."

Chloé was still nodding.

Even before I was a single parent, Chloé's grandmother often took her to the ballet, so she understood dance better than I did. "You knew what was happening on stage, didn't you?" I asked her. "It was ballet that doesn't look like ballet."

She nodded again, "I'm surprised you didn't recognize the Phillip Glass music, Daddy. It's so modern."

"I liked the middle bit, with the monotonous rhythm and musical variations."

"Yes, the music supported the pas de deux perfectly," she said knowingly.

George sat on the edge of his seat to say, "I liked the third section. The pulse of music, pushing all those dancers around, like they were in Grand Central Station or something. Wow."

It was clear that he wasn't used to big theatrical dance pieces. For that matter, neither was I.

Chloé was nodding. "I agree. George. Robbins' choreography is the best."

"Do you know the next choreographer?" George asked.

"Peter Martins? I've seen his *Swan Lake* and *Romeo and Juliet*. He ran NYCB for years, then retired because of sexual assault issues."

My daughter, the feminist, I thought, as the lights went down and the curtain went up for the Martins' ballet.

When the curtain came down, I clapped along with the rest of the audience, but the first dance was better for me than the swan in a black tutu.

The lights came on, and Chloé looked at me. Without turning her head, she took hold of George's hand. "Daddy, I'm going to terminate the pregnancy," she announced without blinking.

I felt my jaw drop. I looked across Chloé at George for confirmation of what I'd heard. He didn't blink either. So, it was a joint decision.

"Why?" I asked. "You're healthy, you're …."

She interrupted me by holding up her hand. "I am not ready to be a parent. I'm carving out my career, I'm not married, and I have 15 years left for having babies, when and if I want."

I pointed at George and opened my mouth to say George would marry her, but she held up her hand again.

"I'll know when I'm ready, Daddy. This is the 21st century; we need to want and cherish our babies, not resent them."

She stopped, and I kept quiet. My heart was racing. Resent a baby? Not have a baby? I had thought that she needed time to get used to the pregnancy, but she had been thinking about abortion all along. No wonder she hadn't wanted me to tell her mother.

"You can be with me on this, Daddy, or not. I hope you're with me, because I need your support."

Beyond my focused field of vision, I saw George nodding in agreement. My mouth opened and closed without anything coming out. Before I could form real words, the lights went out and the curtain rose.

I didn't see much of the third dance. The Wayne Shorter music skipped by my ears and slid over my head.

I didn't say a word while we filed out of the auditorium and collected our coats and umbrellas.

Outside, it was still raining, and I used my heart-attack card to escape: "I'm feeling a little under the weather," I said, patting my chest. "I think I'll take care of myself and go home to bed."

Even in the rain-diffused light in front of the Koch Theater, I could see Chloé's eyebrows go up above her red glasses. I couldn't tell if she was worried about her poor old sick dad, or if she could tell I wanted to escape to chew on her pregnancy decision.

Unfortunately, before I could take a step into Lincoln Center's sprawling patio, George spoke: "You've been sitting a long time, Andy." There it was again, him calling me by my first name like we were friends. "You'll feel better after you move around a little. Go with us to the stage tour. I bet you'll feel better."

He stood on one side of me, Chloé was on the other. Unless I called an ambulance to get me away from them, I was trapped. The three of us moved toward the side of the theater closest to the street.

Ned Lewis was standing under the stage door light looking for us. I reintroduced him to Chloé and presented George, and he led us inside, with a wave at the security guard.

Sweaty dancers were still chatting in the hallway, and musicians with their instruments were heading in the

114

other direction. Ned led us around corners and turns and suddenly we were looking out from the wings on the right side of the stage. There were heavy curtains, with ropes of every size stretched to the ceiling 50 feet above, and wads of wires went into an electrical box the size of an SUV.

"Stagehands are sweeping, but we can go out on the stage if you like," Ned said.

Chloé held George's hand and looked around the audience area in wonder. Its tiers, balconies, aisles, and chandeliers were giant from the stage's perspective.

Ned pointed to the orchestra pit beneath us, and I walked to the edge, looked down, and imagined myself in a musician's chair, not for one of the stringed instruments; no, it would have to be a saxophone. Maybe a clarinet.

I was startled out of my dream when I heard Ned speak next to me: "The dancers take bows, but the musicians are out of the pit and on their way home by the time the audience stops clapping."

"It was a terrific show tonight," I told him. "Thanks for the tickets. My daughter knows about ballet, but me, not so much, and I enjoyed myself completely." The "completely" was a lie, but that wasn't Ned's fault.

"Good," he said, "I'm glad. Now, follow me."

I did as I was told, and with George and Chloé in tow, we ended up where we started, where six people were huddled together just inside the stage door out of the rain.

Ned introduced us to the small group and told us, "After shows, dancers usually go to the Three Monkeys

Bar for beer and nachos. But the musicians," he turned and indicated the group, "the musicians go to Dizzy's."

A skinny man in the group explained, "Because it's close."

A woman with curly brown hair added, "And since we're NYCB musicians, our drinks are free there."

Ned explained, "Dizzy's is in the Jazz at Lincoln Center building."

A man with a paunch stepped past us, saying, "So let's go!"

The small crowd pushed out, opening umbrellas.

I tried to tell Ned I couldn't go, but the crowd chatter swamped him and Chloé as they moved south toward Columbus Circle. I fell back with George and followed.

"You're feeling better, it looks like," George said.

I heard a snicker underneath his words, and it made me mad that my lie had been so transparent.

We fell further behind the crowd when we stopped at a red light at 64th Street.

"You have to know, Andy, that Chloé and I thought about this pregnancy thing a long time. It's not a rash decision. She did research and made lists. We talked and talked, trying to consider everything. After it all, I agreed with her, but finally, it was her choice, and we have to respect it."

I swallowed hard. I did not want to tear up in front of this…this talent agent that my daughter had fallen for.

George went on, "Chloé really regrets the mistake. We both do. You can be sure, it won't happen again."

I wiped my nose with my handkerchief and hoped it looked like I was clearing off dripping raindrops. "Well, you see, George," I began with a throaty voice, "I understand your situation better than you might guess."

He looked at me, straight on, with a question in his eyes. Damn, we were exactly the same height. "Oh yeah? How's that?" he asked.

His eloquence was startling, I thought sarcastically.

I swallowed. "Chloé was a surprise to her mother and me, just like this baby is a surprise to you and Chloé." I felt my knees buckle. I steeled myself. I gritted my teeth. I refused to look weak in front of this man.

The light turned green, and I didn't move.

George cocked his head to the side and said, "You mean, you…"

I nodded. "Yes, Chloé's mother was two months along when she realized she was going to have a baby. It was a shock, but we went ahead like we were supposed to. We got married, and Chloé was born, and I couldn't have been happier. I'm not trying to influence your decision, but I want you to understand my reaction."

"But you're divorced."

It was my turn to cock my head to the side. "Yes."

"Chloé knows of course," he said with a half-question in his voice.

I shook my head. "No. Her mother and I didn't think there was any reason to label her 'an accident.' We wanted the baby. Chloé was not unwanted." I choked, couldn't say any more, and crossed the street right before the light changed again.

George caught up to me on the other side of the intersection. "It wouldn't change her mind if she knew," he said, falling in step with me.

Without looking up, I replied, "And please don't tell her."

§§

When George and I got off the elevator at the 5th floor, we walked into the Saturday night crowd at Dizzy's. I didn't recognize the music, but I blinked twice when I saw that it was Terri Lyne Carrington on drums. Behind the band, the room's panoramic windows showed the city lights through raindrops.

I saw Chloé at a table on the left. She had saved a chair on each side of her for George and me. The woman from the stage entrance with the brown curly hair was on the other side of me and pointed to her chest, speaking over the music, "Shannon Shriver, no relation to Sargent or Maria."

"Andy Brown," I said back.

Across the table, the skinny man from the stage door spoke to me, "I'm Tommy Vickery." He motioned to the waiter to come over and asked, "What'll you have?"

I looked around the table. Chloé was having a beer. Apparently, she didn't care that a pregnant woman shouldn't drink alcohol. Ned Lewis, sitting next to the skinny man, had something clear with ice, vodka maybe. Shannon Shriver had a highball too.

"I'll take a scotch rocks," I said to the waiter.

"You've got to try these cornbread madeleines," Shannon said to Chloé and me, and pushed one of the appetizer plates toward us. "They're fabulous."

"The sweet potato fries are better," Ned proclaimed. "Dip them in the black pepper crème fraiche. They're famous for it here."

Tommy Vickery pointed to his glass for a refill from the waiter. "I can't get enough of Carrington," he said, staring at the woman on drums.

My drink came, and I downed a long swallow that swam down my throat, cruised into my stomach, and said to me, "I am going to save you tonight." It had been a long time since I leaned into the pleasure of good scotch.

"What instrument do you play?" I asked the skinny guy and took another gulp of scotch.

A paunchy man answered, "Tommy's a percussionist."

Skinny Tommy nodded.

"And you?" I asked the paunchy guy, signaling for a second drink.

Chloé gave me a disapproving stare, and said under her breath, "Hard liquor with your medication?"

I ignored her.

"Me, I play flute."

"That's Pete," Tommy said about the big guy who played the tiny instrument.

Good, I thought. Easy to remember: Paunchy Pete.

Tommy gestured around the table, "Harold there, he's bassoon; Roberta, she's our best double bass; Monty plays clarinet; Bobbie is viola; and Shannon plays trumpet."

120

I nodded and laughed, "Shannon Shriver, no relation to Sargent or Maria." These were my kind of people. I enjoyed my rich clients at Bergdorf, and my family was my family, but musicians, yes, they were my clan, even if I'd never joined them.

Around the table, the musicians talked about the dancers and the errors during the evening's show; they riffed on the musical director and then on the rain outside.

I put in my two bits with, "I'm obsessed with these sweet potato fries, Ned."

"I told you they were good. And how about that crème fraiche sauce?"

I signaled the waiter and asked for three more orders of the fries for the table.

Shannon ordered another drink, and Paunchy Pete commanded, "Make it another round for everyone." Then he asked Roberta which candidate in the upcoming election was pro-union.

Through the talking, eating, and drinking, Terri Lyne Carrington's rhythms surrounded us like a warm coat.

After my third drink, I said, "I know one thing for sure, you guys need better lighting outside the stage door."

They agreed, and Shannon said, "You're not the first one to say that. In the last year, there have been two muggings out there."

I laughed, "There was a third one. That was me," I said and pointed to my chest.

"You never told me that," Chloé said, as she took the last sip of her beer.

I nodded, "Oh yes. Right at the corner on the far side of the stage door."

Ned, George, Roberta, Shannon, and Tommy leaned toward me to hear.

"A guy in all black came at me with a knife."

"Jeez, a knife?" Skinny Tommy said, shocked.

"Nobody was around. I didn't know what to do, but something in me took over, and I started dancing wildly, like a crazy person doing a jig on one leg, my arms waving in the air, and I screeched like a hyena. I guess I freaked out the mugger, because he ran away."

Roberta laughed, "I'm going to try that the next time I get in a tight spot. I'll out-crazy the crazy person."

"You were lucky," Ned said seriously, and Shannon bobbed her head up and down, agreeing with him.

"I'm usually lucky," I said happily. I hadn't felt this good in months. Not drunk, just pleasantly high. Without looking at my watch, I decided it was time to go home. "It was great to meet you all. And Ned, what an outstanding night. Thanks, thanks, thanks," I said effusively and stood up. "Are you going uptown?" I asked Chloé.

"I think we'll stay a little longer, Daddy." She looked at me sideways and said, "You're okay getting home?"

I leaned down, kissed her cheek, and felt dizzy. Dizzy! Get it? We were at Dizzy's Jazz, and I was dizzy.

"I'm fine," I lied. "I'll take a cab." With my umbrella in hand, I waved at the crowd as I left.

§§

"I lost 7 pounds this week? Maybe I should drink Scotch more often," I said. "Saturday night, I went out." I was still reeling from the experience.

Ponytail wrapped the blood pressure sleeve around my arm and nonchalantly asked, "What did you do?"

Bedside manner was not Ponytail's strong suit, so I wondered why he was throwing out a chit-chat question. But I answered, "Chloé and I went to the ballet, then to Dizzy's Jazz club with some of the orchestra musicians." I didn't know what to call George: A friend? A partner? A boyfriend? The father of her soon to be aborted child? It was easier not to mention him. I tried to breathe slowly to keep my blood pressure in check.

"You like the ballet?" he asked, sounding skeptical, taking off the BP sleeve.

"Is it lower this week?" I asked in return. "I ate some of the things you said. A couple of bananas. Peanut butter and apricot preserves. No potatoes, but sweet potatoes, lots of sweet potatoes." I envisioned Paunchy Pctc and Shannon no relation-to-Sargent-or-Maria swishing the sweet potato fries in the white sauce. "That's potassium, right?"

"129/75. Lots better than last week, but still high," Ponytail said. "Let's go another week with potassium instead of Enalapril. Yes, sweet potatoes are full of

123

potassium. As for your weight, you can be pleased with your progress. You must be unloading secrets left and right."

Roberta's laugh rang in my memory when she heard my story about scaring away a mugger. Whether I had sounded ridiculous or not, it was a worthy secret to tell. On the other hand, I regretted telling George about my shot-gun wedding. Of all the stupid choices, to tell George. Two secrets, a big night out, and Chloé's revelation about her baby: no wonder I'd lost weight.

Ponytail went on, "I am going to remind you about Xarelto. It's a blood thinner that's supposed to keep your blood flowing with ease. If you have a bloody nose or heavy bruising, let me know." He squinted at me, then looked away to say, "And if you drink a lot, tell me, because alcohol is a natural blood thinner. Combined with Xarelto, it can cause dizziness, weakness, or blurred vision, all warning signs for heart patients."

I chuckled remembering Dizzy's. "Sounds like a good buzz to me. Tipsy, you know, not drunk."

Ponytail pressed his lips together and didn't respond. I guess he figured I was smart enough to hear what he was saying without repeating himself. I didn't defend myself. I'd had a great time in Dizzy's forgetting the reality of my family.

As I was leaving, Ponytail said to my back, "I was at the ballet Saturday night. Shorter's *Emanon* was a great way to end the evening."

I turned around and nodded, as if I had paid attention to the night's third ballet.

§§

Tuesday morning at 8:15, I flagged down a taxi. The driver got out to help me load my big suitcase into the trunk of the yellow cab. At Bergdorf's employee entrance, he lifted the heavy thing out, and I tipped him well. Lucky for me, the suitcase had wheels.

I road the back elevator up to the top floor and found Dominic, sitting in a ray of sunlight streaming in from the window, with a needle in his hand stitching an invisible line along the neckline of a woman's white gown.

He glanced up and grunted, "Andy. You remembered our date. How nice. What have you brought me?"

I couldn't lift the suitcase onto the cutting table at the side of the room, so I knelt down on one knee and opened it on the floor. "These are some of the suits, slacks, and jackets that don't fit anymore. I didn't bother to bring the shirts."

"Let's have a look," he said. Standing up, he was not much taller than me kneeling down. We pulled things out and spread them on the table. He fingered the fabrics and inspected seams, tossing some things back in the suitcase. Then he had me turn around and held three suit coats and three jackets against my back. He found matching pants for each, and he slid everything else off the table onto the floor.

He called to a young woman in an apron at an ironing board and pointed to the floor, "Robin, please fold these things neatly into this suitcase." The words sounded like a request, but the tone was a king speaking to his servant.

With his hand on the table, Dominic looked up at me and said, "I'll alter these pieces, and you'll have a week's worth of work clothes." I didn't bother to ask what the price would be. I'd pay whatever he wanted.

"Come over here, so I can take your measurements," he ordered.

Dominic led me behind a screen to undress. Then I stood on a fitting platform, while he stood on a stool to measure my shoulders, arms, and neck.

In the middle of assessing my upper body, he said, "Andy, you must tell your barber to trim the hair in your ears."

I wanted to melt into the concrete floor from embarrassment. "I trim my nose hair," I told him defensively. He was the first and hopefully the last person in the universe to know that personal grooming detail. "I can do the ears too."

"The barber has a clear view and will do it better," he insisted. As if he hadn't just shattered my self-image, he continued with measurements of my chest, then stepped off his stool to put the tape around my waist and hips, and along the ins-seam and legs.

"I'll have these ready for you by Friday afternoon," Dominic said. He looked at his watch and added, "You have an hour before the opening bell. Go to the Men's Store and buy slacks, sport coats, and shirts before you go to work."

I put my clothes back on, saying, "Thank you, Dominic. Thank you. You're a savior."

"Thank me on Friday when you see the transformations I do." He crossed his arms across his chest and smiled. "And you can tip me with a tester of Tom Ford's *Fucking Fabulous Eau de Parfum*."

"You'll have it today," I promised.

He reached out, unbuckled my belt, and slid it out of the loops. "I'll shorten this. Buy a new one before you step on the sales floor."

I rolled the half-empty suitcase with one hand and held up my pants with the other to head to the elevator. I stowed the bag and was on my way to the employee exit when it occurred to me to swing by the jewelry department. Frank Bryson was polishing the glass counter, looking dapper in a navy blazer with a maroon tie on top of a pale yellow shirt. I'd look good in that combination.

I kept a hand on waist of my trousers and said, "Hi, Frank. I've got a question for you."

He looked up and continued polishing. "I'm ready," he said.

"I've lost some weight. Does that mean my ring size may have changed?"

He put the rag down, looked over his half-moon glasses and nodded. "It certainly does. I can measure your ring finger if you want."

128

I stuck out my left hand, fingers spread. "I'd appreciate it."

He pulled out a collection of metal rings, slid one on my finger, and shook his head. He tried another, and then a third. "You're a 9½. You were a 10 before, right?"

I nodded.

"The weight loss…, is everything okay? I mean, after your heart attack?"

"I'm doing okay," I told him. "Just slimming down some." I didn't take time to try on my Son of Poseidon ring. "Thanks for the measurement," I said and rushed to the Men's Store.

§§

I promised myself not to tell Ponytail that I arrived in the Perfume Department out of breath as the opening bell rang.

Faith stared at me like she was seeing Santa Claus. "You look like you stepped out of *Vogue Magazine*," she said.

I grinned and did my best imitation of a model showing off on a runway, with my arms out, turning 360° around. There was no need for me to hold onto the waist of my new navy blue Armani trousers because my new Magnanni calf leather belt was doing its job.

Ryker came over from stocking the other side of our display and gave me the once over with his eyebrows raised. "Is there a new woman in your life you haven't told us about?"

"I do look good, don't I?" I responded with a laugh. "And you should see the four bags of new clothes I left at the security desk to pick up later. I am going to GQ the world!"

"You are a star," Faith said, touching the subtle plaid fabric of the sport coat.

"It's Zegna," I said. "Cashmere and silk, and on sale!"

Ryker looked impressed. "I should go over to the men's store and see what they have on sale in my size."

Faith leaned in close, "And what size are you now, my dear Andy?"

I couldn't get the grin off my face. "I'll never tell, except to say that I haven't tried on clothes like this in decades. I found an Armani suit in dark brown virgin wool, on sale; it's being altered. And I bought 2 sport coats, 3 trousers, and 4 shirts." I preened. "It's my old tie, but how do you like the yellow shirt? I got navy, light blue, and peach too."

Ryker looked me up and down and said, "I have some 'work' to do in the stock room. I'll be back before lunch."

Faith raised one eyebrow and answered him, "We'll take care of all your customers while you're shopping across the street. After lunch, it'll be my turn to shop the sales on the sixth floor." She waved her hands to shoo Ryker away, "Go!" Then she turned to me, "You do look good, Andy."

A glow warmed me inside. I think it came from feeling proud of myself and my new look. "Dominic Berlini upstairs is altering some of my other clothes."

"With him doing the work, it'll be like you have new suits," Faith said. She opened the drawer under the cash register and said, "You better keep him happy," shoveling me a batch of samples.

I put the samples in a bag and replied, "I have to do more than this. He specifically requested a tester of *Fucking Fabulous*."

She giggled, "I can't sell that cologne. It's too hard for me to say the 'F' word in public."

I poked her in the ribs, "I've heard you say it in private often enough."

Two women walked toward us: one wore an orange bomber jacket, jeans, and high heels, and I mean, *high* heels; the other was blond underneath a cowboy hat that went well with her fringed shirt and blue jeans. Faith and I exchanged the same look we gave each other several times a day, a look that said, "This one is mine." But usually, we stood at our perspective spots behind the counter and waited to see the direction a customer drifted. This time it was to Faith. That was okay with me. There was always another customer… if we didn't count the months BG closed its doors for Covid.

I spent the next stretch of time admiring myself in the mirrors behind the glass display shelves. I looked young in my new yellow shirt and plaid sport coat. I'd have to get a haircut in the next couple of days, and I'd find a way to ask for the hair in my ears to be clipped, despite my shame and embarrassment.

I glanced away from my reflection when a man approached the counter. He was tallish, around my age, and completely bald. I didn't recognize him, but five steps away, I spotted Tom Ford's rectangular stainless steel watch on his right wrist. It wasn't the most expensive watch available, but with its pearl grey alligator band, it was distinctive. So, the man had money, was left handed, and most probably had a flashy car waiting for him somewhere nearby.

He walked directly toward me, and I stood straight in order that my 5'9" appeared confident, with my hands folded on the counter.

"Hello," I greeted him simply. I didn't believe in offering help or asking what a customer needed. Anyone with a shred of intelligence could tell I was waiting to be of service.

"Nice shirt," the man said.

"Thank you," I said, giving him a smile of appreciation, and I silently thanked Frank Bryson in jewelry for the yellow shirt idea.

Then the customer threw out the opening gambit: "My wife's birthday is tomorrow. I need a few special things for her."

"I have some ideas for you," I answered. In 15 minutes, I knew his name, Charles O'Donnell, a dermatologist who owned a brownstone on East 69th Street, married to his wife Chris for 21 years, waiting for his second child to finish Princeton so he and Chris could travel more.

I presented four scents. I never did more than that. More were intimidating and confusing. He liked the Roja Amber Aoud. It was not a shy fragrance, with its top notes of lime and bergamot, heart notes of fig and jasmine, and a sexy base of oakmoss, ambergris, and musk. Obviously, he was not a shy man, and probably the same would be said for his wife Chris.

He didn't ask the price when I showed him the one fluid ounce of parfum absolue. Then I suggested the rejuvenating body crème in the same fragrance. He shrugged agreement, and I asked for his credit card.

I was turning away toward the cash machine when I paused, held up a finger as if something surprising had occurred to me, and opened a cabinet where the Roja Reed Diffuser was on display. "You might want to look at this also, Mr. O'Donnell. It's a Lalique Crystal decanter for perfume diffusers. I have your Amber Aoud fragrance in reed oil for scenting the home."

"Chris loves those sticks that make the air smell good," O'Donnell said. "May I see them?"

I pulled out the Lalique decanter, three bottles of oil necessary to fill the decanter, and the collection of diffuser sticks to put in the decanter.

O'Donnell was smiling and said, "Yes, she'll love it. Wrap it all together and have it sent over to my address tomorrow." He handed me a business card, and I started ringing up.

He scribbled his signature on the receipt for $9,800, and said, "Tuck in a note with the delivery that says, 'Do Not Open Until Chuck Gets Home.' And of course, don't include the price tag."

"I'll take care of everything, Mr. O'Donnell. Here's my card. Call me if you need anything else." My BG business card was now in the hands of a lovely man who was a big spender. I put out my hand to shake on our new relationship.

After Charles O'Donnell was gone, I logged the sale in my pocket notepad, with details about the customer, and the notation to call him the next week to see if his wife was pleased with the Roja scent.

When I looked up, Faith was smiling.

"You made a sale too?" I asked.

"Oh yes sir," she said happily.

Ryker was business-like about his sales. But Faith and I both took pleasure in selling. It wasn't just the big commission from a big sale, although neither of us objected to receiving a good paycheck. No, it was satisfying to connect with a customer and gratifying to know his delight was because of me. I had searched for ways to make Charles O'Donnell happy, I had read his personality correctly, and I had pleased him. It was the definition of an enjoyable work experience.

That sale and my new lucky yellow shirt boded well for a good day.

§§

"Your daughter has always been the best at everything," Nana said. "You know that about her, Andy. She's hyper-everything. She works hard and loves hard. She's creative and intellectual at the same time."

"She's not a rocket scientist, Nana. She's a physical therapist."

We were having breakfast at Barney Greengrass on Amsterdam Avenue. In the old days, we would have met at Popover's with Chloé before she went to school on the crosstown bus. Nana always told my daughter that a popover with strawberry jam and butter was the recipe for making A's in school. But Popover's had closed when the owner retired ten years ago. Chloé never stopped making A's at Eleanor Roosevelt High School, and she kept on with her good grades in college.

"She's the most intense person I know," Nana said.

"We must know different people, because my Chloé is gentle and happy, no matter what."

She took a bite of her poppyseed bagel with lox, tomato, and cream cheese. I didn't understand how an old woman like my mother stayed small eating the way she did. I was eating the same breakfast, and I was fat. Less fat than before, but fat.

"She told you about her new project?" Nana goaded me.

"Which one, the one about eczema?"

She wiggled her eyebrows, delighted to be ahead of me on news about Chloé. "No, more recent than that. Ask her. She'll be glad to tell you."

"Where does she come up with her strange ideas? It's not like they have anything to do with her work." I signaled the waiter for a coffee refill.

"It's always her work," Nana said. "A patient breaks both legs in a motorcycle accident, and something clicks in her brain that sets her off on a tangent about cloud formation. It's the way her mind operates."

I shook my head in wonder, "Like when she invented the new dog leash because of a patient who was a Yankees pitcher."

"The leash which Blue loves."

"And which is easier on your arm. Is your shoulder still bothering you?"

Nanette shrugged, "The bursitis doesn't stop my painting. That's what matters."

I looked at my watch. "I need to go, Nana." I picked up the check.

"I'll pay," she said.

I smirked, stood up, and took out my wallet. "No."

She looked at me sideways and smiled. "Okay. But I'm paying for something, and you don't know about it yet. Well, actually, Cary's paying for it. It's going to be a grand surprise."

I could tell she was teasing me, goading my curiosity, instead of speaking outright. Whatever it was, she'd never tell me until she was ready, so I ignored her bait.

"Cary's doing okay?" I asked, sliding into my new sport coat.

She took a sip of coffee, then answered me sarcastically, "Cary's at the gym doing gyrations with Ned Lewis, as usual."

"Don't complain. It keeps him in shape for you." I started to leave, then sat down again on the edge of the chair to ask softly, "Has Chloé scheduled the abortion?"

Nana eyed me over the top of her glasses. "You'll have to ask her yourself. It's her story to tell, not mine."

"I told George that Tanya was pregnant when I married her. I'm hoping he doesn't tell Chloé."

She took hold of my hand as if I were a little boy. "Andy, how stupid can you be?"

"You're right. I shouldn't have said it. As soon as the words were out of my mouth, I could have kicked myself."

Nana rolled her eyes. "I don't mean stupid about telling George. I mean, Chloé has known forever that she was the reason you and Tanya got married. It doesn't take a genius to subtract your wedding date from her birthday five months later."

I didn't have a reply. Chloé knew she was an accident? I was stunned.

Nana tugged on my hand and pulled me close to kiss my cheek. "Have a good day, darling. Call me soon."

I left in a daze. Chloé knew? Well, it didn't seem to make any difference to her, not about herself, and not about her pregnancy. "So maybe you should let it go," I told myself out loud. Only one pedestrian passing by took note of me talking to myself.

I calculated the distance from Barney Greengrass on Amsterdam and 86th to Mount Sinai West on 56th and 8th Avenue. I looked at the blue sky, then at my watch again, and decided I'd give it a try on foot.

At Lincoln Center, I sat on the bench in front of the Juilliard School, a bench I had become friendly with since my heart attack. After a couple of minutes resting, I kept on walking and finally knocked on Ponytail's door 10 minutes early for the appointment.

I let the nurse practitioner run his routine tests and make his routine notes. He didn't comment on my 225 pounds or on my new clothes, and sent me on my way.

§§

Work felt routine too: clients, sales, stocking products, breaks. The only interesting detail was Ryker presenting us with a new perfume from Boadiciea the Victorious, an expensive citrus fragrance called Blue Sapphire.

I ignored the new rollerball perfume Wisteria Blue he showed us, not because it was cheap, but the whole rollerball thing reminded me of deodorants. That and the "hair perfume craze" irritated me. In fact, everything irritated me.

"Oh for that…," I told a customer who asked me about Estee Lauder, "… you should speak to Faith. She's the expert for those fragrances." I said it with an elegant wave toward my blond colleague.

"You're crabby today, Andy," Faith told me after she made the sale. "What's up? You don't like the new clothes anymore?"

I sneered. "I'm prickly, that's all. I need a change."

"It happens," Ryker said. "A person can serve rich people for only so long without getting pissed off now and again."

"That's not it," I barked. "I have plenty of money. I have everything I want."

They both stared at me like I was crazy.

"Okay, maybe I don't have everything I want, but I'm happy, damn it."

Ryker laughed at me, and I felt my face turn red and my hands clinch up. He took a step back but kept chuckling.

Faith put her hand on my shoulder, and I jerked backwards. "Andy!" she sputtered.

A client came to the counter, spritzed herself with Guerlain's Samsara, and left.

"I hate people like her," I muttered. "All she does all day is shop. Why can't she work like normal people?"

Ryker went to his side of the perfume space, still smiling. Faith did not reach out to touch me again, but she said, "I get envious too, Andy. It's okay. You've been in that pit before, and you'll come out, like we all do."

I didn't reply. Instead I went into the stockroom and paced back and forth. I should've had enough walking already, but I couldn't calm down. "What would you do if you didn't work?" I asked myself. "Play golf? Play poker? Yeah, right," I scoffed. In a sarcastic whiny voice I said, "Maybe you'd volunteer at homeless shelters."

I had worked for more than 30 years, and what did I have to show for it? Nothing!

Faith came in and sat on a carton. "When I get jealous, I tell myself what my father used to say: Don't compare other people's outsides to your insides. That's good, huh? Their outsides, my insides. He was a smart man. A poor man, but smart."

I sneered. This from a woman who lived with her mother because she couldn't afford an apartment after decades of working. Yes, Faith had a problem with buying. Some people would say she was a shopping addict: Hermes scarves, Valentino purses, Chanel jackets, Gucci sweaters.

I took a breath and told myself that Faith was a good woman trying to be nice to me. Out loud, I said, "Okay, I'm furious at the world. I don't know why it hit me today."

She nodded. "You've had a heart attack. You're allowed." She stood up. "Stay here for a while. Or better, go out for a walk. We'll keep things going until you get back," she said and left me alone.

I knew she meant "back to your real self." She was right. If I smoked cigarettes, I'd have an excuse to go outside for a break. "Fuck it," I said and went to the employee exit.

I walked to 59th Street and into Central Park. The peonies were out, joggers were out, bikers were out, and I was out. My daughter was dating a jerk who was letting her have an abortion, my mother was a wise-cracking artist with a huge apartment, my ex-wife was a Hollywood asset, and I was… what was I?

The benches were full of people enjoying the mild weather under leafed-out trees. I walked past a hot dog stand and whiffed the aroma of sauerkraut, the absolute opposite to the perfume smells at my counter. The irony made me laugh, and I turned back.

It would be nice to be rich. By that I meant rich-rich, not just wealthy or well-to-do. I'd buy a plane that would take me to my private islands and to casinos around the world. I'd invite jazz players to my Italian villa for concerts for me and my friends, and afterwards the staff would serve us lobster as an appetizer followed by duck à l'orange with sparkling wine.

But reality was different. I was a working man with a grown daughter, not a multi-millionaire. I had to accept it and continue my life as it was, but I felt my lip curl into a snarl at the thought.

Heading back to Bergdorf's, at the 59th Street light, I said out loud, "I need a hobby."

The other people waiting for the light to change didn't offer me suggestions.

The week slipped by, and I slowly rose out of my funk. Thursday night after work, I deposited all my change in the blue crystal vase on my dresser, and this time, a couple of dimes spilled over the edge.

"Great," I said to my empty apartment, "Tonight's the night."

I turned on the T.V. and searched Amazon Prime for a good movie. It was between *Dark Waters* and *Bohemian Rhapsody*. I liked Robert Bilott, but I decided high energy *Don't Stop Me Now* music would be a better background for counting money. I fixed myself a diet coke with fresh lemon, brought in the box of coin wrappers, settled onto the couch with the blue vase on the coffee table, and started the movie.

By the time the vase was half empty, I had to get up and take a piss. By the time it was bare, I was starving, but I counted the rolls of coins before I ate: $871 in quarters, dimes, nickels, and pennies.

I lugged the gym bag from the bottom of my closet and added the rolls of coins to the others in the bag, making a grand total of $2948. Only $1052 more to be able to buy the Son of Poseidon ring. I whistled *Crazy Little Thing Called Love* the whole time I cooked pasta and asparagus for dinner.

§§

"Vous êtes très belle aujourd'hui," I told Ms. Handley when she approached the counter. I had regained my selling rhythm. Nothing had changed, except the days had passed and my moral climbed.

"Merci beaucoup," Ms. Handley replied, in a terrible French accent, even worse than mine. "I got back from my trip on Tuesday," she bubbled.

"And I am sure that all of Paris was sorry to see you leave," I told her. "But for me, your return is a pleasure."

Ms. Handley was an older woman, probably in her late 70's, with rather bright red hair, bright red lipstick, and a bright red belt around the rather wide waist of her black dress. She was always smiling, and I loved her for it.

She leaned in close, and I could smell her Gardenia Petale by Van Cleef & Arpels. "We've been together for 20 years, you and I, Mr. Brown. Can you believe it?"

I patted her hand and said "It seems like a moment. A glorious moment, but it has gone quickly. Tell me about your trip."

She chatted on about seeing "l'exposition *La Collection Morozov. Icônes de l'art moderne*" at the Fondation Louis Vuitton." Clearly, she enjoyed dropping French words into our conversation, as if it made her vacation go on longer.

145

I tried to assist by saying, "Ma belle, c'est comme je peux voir les tableaux Morozov when you describe them." It was the best I could do after three years of French in high school and two at college.

"Oh, your French is impeccable," she swooned. "It's one of the reasons je vous adore."

I winked at her and whispered, "I can count to 10 in ten different languages, but I can only speak English."

"No!" she gasped. "Ten languages? You must show me!"

Truthfully, I'd never told anyone that detail about myself. The numbers seemed like useless information stored in my head, but the news delighted Ms. Handley. I walked around to the customer side of the counter and took her by the arm. She was stooped, but she had a light step, and her eyes sparkled as if I were taking her on a Disneyland adventure.

I escorted her slowly around the Beauty Level of Bergdorf's, more commonly known as the basement, counting: "un, deux, trois, quatre, cinq, six, sept," and Ms. Handley joined with me for, "huit, neuf, dix."

She laughed and said, "My French. Oh it's a wonderful language. What's next?"

"You'll recognize this too," I said. "Uno, due, tre, quattro, cinque, sei, sette, otto, nove, dieci."

"I don't know Italian myself, but I recognize the sound of it. It's lovely when you say it."

146

That was a lie, I was certain, but I accepted the lie graciously and went on. "Ins, zwei, drei, vier, fünf, sechs, sieben, acht, neun, zehn."

"I'm just guessing," she said, "but German, yes?"

I squeezed her arm. "Quite right. Here's a more difficult one," I said as we passed by the Bobbi Brown counter. "Yī, èr, sān, sì, wǔ, liù, qī, bā, jiǔ, shí. I won't make you guess that one. It's Mandarin Chinese." I went on as we walked, "Uno, dos, tres, cuatro, cinco, seis, siete, ocho, nueve, diez."

"Spanish," she said. "I know it from the Latinos speaking on the street here."

"You are absolutely correct," I told her. "And now, Danish: En, To, Tre, Fire, Fem, Seks, Syv, Otte, Ni, and Ti."

"Ah, I remember Copenhagen. It's been years since I went to Denmark, but I loved it," she sighed.

We passed the La Prairie corner, and I said, "Um, dois, três, quatro, cinco, seis, sete, oito, nove, dez."

She pulled on my arm to stop me. "You've already done Spanish. You can't count it twice."

I smiled, "Yes, but that was Portuguese. Very close to Spanish, and Italian too. Now I'm going to count in Russian. You'll have to forgive me; I know my pronunciation is far from correct."

She started walking again. "I won't know if it's good or bad."

"Odin, dva, tri, chetyre, pyat, shest, sem, vosem, devyat, desyat. And here's a fun one; it's Irish: uh-Aon, uh-

Do, uh-Tri, uh-Ceathair, uh-Cuig, uh-Sé, uh-Seacht, uh-Ocht, uh-Naoi, and uh-Deich."

"You are so remarkable, Mr. Brown. You must come with me on my next trip!"

She had suggested this through the years, but I knew nothing about these languages beyond a few superficial words, so I always agreed with her and never followed through on the offer.

"That's nine, and here we are again at the perfume counter."

She smiled, showing perfect teeth which must have been dentures, I thought. "What's the last language going to be?" she asked.

I gave a bow from the waist with my palms together and said, "hitotsu, futatsu, mittsu, yottsu, itsutsu, muttsu, nanatsu, yattsu, kokonotsu, tou."

Ms. Handley bowed back and said, "Japanese."

"Again, my pronunciation is laughable," I apologized. I let go of her arm and went behind the counter, smiling.

"How did you ever learn all of that?" she asked.

I felt myself blush, but I told her, "When I divorced, I fell into obsessive habits, and one of those was counting. I counted stairs when I went up, I counted brush strokes when I brushed my teeth…, well, I could go on and on. I couldn't seem to stop counting. Anyhow, I decided to put the obsession to good use and began counting in other languages."

"What a wonderful story!" Ms. Handley said.

148

"Finally, the obsession disappeared," I sighed. "You have been a delightful audience for my secret showing off." That was no sales pitch. I meant it. She had listened as if I was telling her how to get to the end of the rainbow. She was the kind of person I wished I were, vital, attentive, and open.

"It's always a pleasure to spend time with you, Mr. Brown." She looked at me coyly, "You'll send along my regular order to my apartment?"

"It will be delivered as usual to your doorman around 10 a.m. tomorrow morning," I answered, taking her hand again and holding it in both of mine on the counter. "Are you jet-lagged?" I asked.

She smiled and nodded. "A bit. But I had to come see you. And now, nap time!" Ms. Handley let me hold her hand an instant longer, and then left with a smile.

It took me less than a half-hour to collect her usual make-up and perfume products, charge them to her account that I guarded in my book, and personally carry them to the shipping department. Yes, a nice commission, and a pleasure too.

§§

When I called Chloé after breakfast, George answered.

"She's in the shower, Andy," he told me.

"I want to talk to her," I said simply.

He must have been looking at the computer because it took him a second to respond. "Ah, yeah. Can I do something for…. Oh wait. Listen to this."

A loud male voice came through the phone, a voice talking about DraftKings and Fantasy Football, "bragging rights Monday morning," and so forth.

George's voice came back on the line. "That's my client, right there, making a fortune for himself and for me on radio. He does on-line ads too. I knew he had it the first time he contacted me…a little lisp, like he has too much spit, but hey, the quintessential middle class working guy," George said.

"Could you have Chloé call me back?" I asked.

"Sorry, I got distracted. What is it that you want, Andy?"

I tried to like the guy. Really. "I just want to confirm her appointment today and to see how she's doing."

"Oh you mean about terminating Touchdown?"

Was he still talking about fantasy football? "Touchdown?"

150

He laughed, "Yeah, that's what I call the little guy. 'Fetus' is too clinical for me."

I held the phone away from my ear and closed my eyes.

"But yeah," George continued, "everything's on track for today at 2:00. I'm going with her; she's taking the afternoon off from work. We should be back here in time for *Cold Case* at 3:00."

"Tell her I called," I said and hung up.

I left my apartment, chewing over the conversation. "She loves him," I reminded myself.

On the sidewalk, I walked like I wanted to get away from a fire, fast and aggressively, so fast that I arrived at Mount Sinai 15 minutes before my appointment with Ponytail and plopped in the chair outside his office. I was still replaying the phone exchange in my head when the nurse practitioner opened his door. Another patient left and I went in.

"Today, let's weigh you first," Ponytail said, as if that was a major change in our schedule.

We both stared at the scale's readout: 218

"What do you think about that?" he asked me.

"Another day, another dollar," I answered. As soon as I said it, I knew it didn't make any sense. "I mean, that's good. I feel good."

"And you look good," he said walking to his desk without looking at me.

He jotted his proverbial notes and continued with the exam. "Your blood pressure is good today," he announced.

Aha! That proved that blood pressure readings were bullshit. My blood should have been boiling because of George Kuykendall and "Touchdown."

Ponytail tapped my back, told me to breathe deeply and then to cough, listened to my chest, and said, "I read the new article Chloé sent me. It's very good."

My brain suddenly switched its focus from George to the present moment. "Which article was that?" I asked, as if I was up-to-date on everything my daughter did.

He pulled a folder out of his drawer. "It's just a copy of what she submitted. The note said it was accepted and will be published in the next issue of the *Journal of Human Evolution*."

I opened the folder and read silently, *Presbyopia in the Elderly: In Defense of Love.*

Ponytail was nodding and massaging his chin. "Yes, an insightful and imaginative proposition," he said.

I took a guess and leapt into the conversation, "In an anthropology journal, hummm."

"I'm glad to be on your daughter's mailing list. Vision problems after 50, an evolutionary detail which blinds us from seeing the devastation of aging in beloved partners -- I never would have thought of such an idea."

I nodded, wondering which of her PT patients had inspired the article. "That's Chloé for you."

Ponytail looked at me directly. "You must be proud of her."

I took the first real breath of my day. "Yes," I responded. "I am very proud of her."

§§

I showed up at Chloé's building at 7:00 p.m. with two sacks of groceries, and climbed up the three flights of steps to her apartment. Outside her door, I huffed and puffed and wondered how an ambulance driver would get me down the stairs if I had another heart attack.

Finally, I knocked, and Nana opened the door.

"How's she doing?" I whispered.

"I'm fine, Daddy. Come on in," I heard Chloé call from the living room.

With Cary next to her in a chair, my daughter was stretched out on the couch holding the TV remote control. She muted the sound.

I set the bags down and sat down on the edge of the couch. "I'm so glad to see you, honey."

Chloé took my hand without saying a word. She looked pale and tired. Her spiky hair drooped, and she wasn't wearing her red glasses.

I tried to be light-hearted. "I wanted to bring you a bottle of vodka to make you feel better, but the articles on-line said it wouldn't be good for you."

"Nana's not letting me have beer either. How's a person supposed to survive?" she said with a weak smile. "I threw up a while ago."

George walked into the little living room from the back, carrying a heating-pad and extension cord. "Here you

154

go, Chloé." He plugged the pad in and stretched the cord over the back of the couch. "Now you'll feel better." He looked up at me, shrugged, and added, "I thought she'd be running up the steps after the procedure."

I said to Chloé, "You'll need a few days to get back to normal. I read there'd be cramps, fatigue, bleeding, and lots of feelings. A healthy diet will be half the cure, so I'm making dinner." I looked around and added, "There should be enough for everyone."

"Nanette and I won't eat, Andy," Cary said.

"But I'll help in the kitchen, son," Nana said.

I kissed Chloé's forehead and went to the kitchen with the grocery sacks.

Nana spoke in a soft voice as I set things on the counter. "You'll convince her to take at least one more day off work? Two or three would be better, at least until her breasts stop leaking milk."

I was squeamish about leaking milk as a topic of conversation with my mother and daughter, but I said, "I'll do my best."

I took out a big frying pan, poured in some olive oil, and put in three salmon steaks. Then I threw in a mound of fresh spinach and added salt, pepper, and walnuts. While that cooked on a low heat, I cut up the white cheddar cheese from Fairway and arranged it on a plate with the sliced Swiss Muesli Roll from Bread's Bakery.

"You've got lots of iron and vitamins here," Nana said, looking at the spread.

I nodded and was swamped by something that made me turn to mush. I leaned on the counter and cried.

Nana patted my back. "She's your baby. I know; I know."

I coughed and sniffed. "She looks so fragile in there, and there's nothing I can do about it." I wiped my eyes, but the tears kept shaking me up.

"You're here. That's all she needs."

The heaves slowed down

"You brought fresh mint," Nana said. "I must have raised you right."

I choked and swallowed. "You were a tyrant," I said lightly and picked up a wooden fork to flip the salmon.

"I was fabulous," she said happily. "Do you want me to pour seltzer and add the mint?"

I nodded, still staring at the frying pan. "I love you, Nana."

"And I am very proud of you for supporting Chloé's decision."

I looked at her. "She must have had her reasons."

Nana smiled, "I am sure of it. You think she'll be mad if Cary and I have a glass of wine in front of her while you three eat?"

"Would it make any difference if she did?"

Her smile got bigger. "Not a bit."

§§

Still stretched out on the couch twenty minutes later, Chloé balanced a plate on her lap, while George and I ate from the coffee table.

"Daddy, this is good."

I nodded. "Glad you like it. Eat what you want. I didn't know how hungry you'd be."

"Me, I'm starving, Andy, and it tastes great," George said, cutting another big bite of salmon.

"Have you called your mother yet?" Nana asked Chloé.

I choked on a walnut and took a chug of seltzer to clear my throat.

Chloé's expression matched mine, as if she'd swallowed a golf ball without chewing. "No," she said simply.

"She thinks that her mother will figure it all out in time," George said, making a mini-sandwich from the bread and cheese.

"I've been busy. I haven't had a chance to call her back since she said she was changing her flight for the birth."

That was a fib; I could always see through Chloé's lies. "Humph. She wouldn't have known anything if it hadn't been for my big mouth."

"Will she change her flight again to watch you two moving in together?" Nana said.

Chloé rolled her eyes as if the thought irritated her. Hormones must have been pumping through her wildly, because usually she was super-vigilant to be fair and kind when the subject of Tanya came up.

"I'll call her in the next day or two, and we'll find a time for her to visit," Chloé said. "There's no rush. If I'm feeling back to normal, George thinks he'll bring his things over at the end of next week."

"Or the beginning of the week after," George said. "My landlady doesn't care because I'm paid up until the end of the month. I've already listed a lot of stuff to sell on VarageSale and E-bay. I should be able to fit my clothes and computer crap in a taxi."

Chloé handed her half-eaten plate of food to Cary. "That's all I can manage," she said.

"You did great," Cary replied. "All due to your father's good cooking."

"I taught him everything he knows," Nana said with a straight face, but everyone else in the room laughed at the idea of Nanette Brown doing more in a kitchen than pouring drinks and putting plates in a dishwasher.

"You'll have leftovers," Cary said, setting the plate on the coffee table.

"Which you can have for lunch, because I already have your dinner menu set for tomorrow night," I said.

Chloé's eyes were drooping, like a puppy falling asleep.

Cary stood up, put George's empty plate underneath Chloé's, and said softly, "Tell me about it in the kitchen, Andy."

Scraping scraps into the trash can, he went on, "I'm assuming that George will help her with breakfast tomorrow. Nanette and I will come over to make her lunch. Do you need help with the meal tomorrow night?"

"I should be able to manage, Cary. I'll buy oysters on my way over here for her appetizer, and I'll cook her a chicken omelet."

"Hummm, if you need extra eaters, let me know. I'll be here in a flash."

"You should come and take advantage of the situation. I don't cook the fancy stuff for myself. And I've ordered a walnut cake from Bread's Bakery."

He dried his hands on the dishtowel. "You're looking good, Andy. The stents must be working well."

I grinned. "I'm looking good because I bought new clothes and had some of my old ones altered."

"So you've lost weight," he said. It wasn't a question.

"Around 50 pounds," I replied.

Cary smiled and patted me on the back. "Then you deserve new clothes."

I frowned and turned away, embarrassed. "The clothes cover up how ugly I am. I wouldn't want anyone to see me naked."

Cary had been my substitute father for almost 40 years, but I'd been an adult for a long time. I didn't share private things with him, generally speaking. I trusted him to take care of Nana and left it at that. I didn't know why I had said the thing about being naked.

"You're not ugly, Andy," he said, crossing his arms over his chest.

"Oh yes. I'm ashamed of the folds of loose skin hanging everywhere. I can't say which is worse, the old fat body or the new baggy body."

Cary chuckled and put his hand on my shoulder. "I can't tell you, Andy. You'll have to ask a woman."

"Humph," I grunted. "Fat chance of that. Get it? Fat chance?"

"I got it," he laughed.

"Are you dieting?" Ponytail asked me.

I shook my head No.

"Good," he said. "That means your body is re-calibrating on its own. You're at 210 pounds."

I wanted to talk about Chloé abortion, but I knew he wasn't the one to tell. Not Ryker or Faith either. Chloé would be appalled if I told my colleagues anything more about her personal life. Nana? No, that would be old news.

"Your blood pressure is holding steady," he said after the reading. "When is your check-up with the cardiologist?"

I brought my mind back to the present. "Uh," I tried to remember, "uh, three more weeks, I think."

"I'm writing your refill prescription for a month. Just the Xarelto, not the Enalapril. But I'm going to take another blood sample. Please roll up your sleeve."

He tied elastic around my arm, I made a fist, and he sucked out three syringes of my blood. Blood tests were a barbaric practice, like a witch doctor burning sage or weaving worms into your hair, all in the name of knowledge and healing.

"Nice shirt," Ponytail said, as I unrolled and re-buttoned the sleeve of my new peach-colored poplin Ralph Lauren, $329; final markdown of 75%; minus the employee discount of 25%. My price: $62. The man nurse and I both had good taste.

§§

"I can't believe you didn't tell me," Andy said.

Cary grinned like a Cheshire cat and leaned across the perfume counter to say softly, "Do you remember when I couldn't go to Chloé's first appointment with Dr. Perkins?"

I remembered too well the day with my mother and daughter when Chloé's pregnancy was confirmed. "You had bank business or something."

His eyes sparkled, but it was Nana who answered, "That was the morning he talked to his buddies at PNB Bank about financing the apartment."

Ryker exchanged a look with me to confirm he could have the client entering the perfume department, even though it was my turn.

Nana went on, "It was only a few days after poor Amy Motheral next door tried to kill herself."

"When she went to live with her parents in New Jersey, I had a sneaking feeling the apartment would go on the market," Cary said. "For years, I've wanted Chloé to own an apartment, instead of throwing her money away on rent."

"It turned out, he didn't need a mortgage," Nanette proclaimed. "Cary arranged it all."

"I liquidated a few investments," Cary said shyly. "Of course the Co-Op Board approved Chloé immediately."

"The apartment belongs to Chloé no strings attached," Nana announced, beaming with pride.

Cary chuckled, "Except for the monthly maintenance fee. She has to pay that. It's not much different from rent except it's an investment."

Chloé joined us at the counter and held her hand out to me. "How do you like this fragrance on me?" she asked.

I sniffed and nodded, "Yes. Peonia Nobile. George will love it. But wait until it dries to see how the base notes sit on you." I looked at her sideways, "I hear that you may have more than a new perfume."

Her tinkling laugh danced toward me. Seeing her laugh again filled my heart so much I thought I'd have to run to the stockroom and cry. The difference between her demeanor now and three weeks before was so dramatic that it dawned on me how profoundly Chloé had suffered under the weight of her pregnancy termination. I felt stupid that I had been so focused on myself that I hadn't recognized her anguish before and after the procedure.

"Can you imagine? Cary and Nana giving me an apartment? Right there next to theirs? I'm so lucky!" She leaned in close, "I had to promise never to do what their neighbor did," and she laughed out loud again, as if her committing suicide was ridiculous.

"It was a selfish gift," Cary said. "We're going on a short vacation, and we'll need someone to babysit Blue."

164

Chloé winked at me, "They're spending their anniversary weekend in Block Island."

"Another year of fabulous life together," Nanette said.

"37 years, and she still won't marry me," Cary laughed.

Faith came up to our cluster of four and hugged Chloé. "Oh, it's been too long since you've come by," she cooed. "Turn around," and she held Chloé's hand high for a twirl. "Oh, you are as beautiful as ever. Isn't she, Andy, so beautiful? I love your red glasses, Chloé."

Chloé smiled demurely and murmured a thank you.

Faith held up her palms and commanded, "Don't go anywhere!" She pulled out a Bergdorf bag and filled it with perfume samples from the drawer under the cash register. "I'll get more from Joe Malone, Sisley, and Bobbi Brown," and she scurried off.

"When your colleague gets back, we want you to come with us to the Home department. Chloé needs new bedding for the new apartment," Nana said.

"And towels and dishes," Cary said. "Nanette's list is endless."

Nana pointed at me, "Your contribution to this generous gift is going to be your employee discount."

Chloé laughed, and I didn't argue.

Faith came back and handed my daughter a giant bag of samples and kissed her on both cheeks.

"I promise I'll come by more often," Chloé said smiling. Then she went to the other side of the department

165

where Ryker was talking to a middle-aged client. "Excuse me, ma'am," she said with a glowing smile. "I just have to kiss this man. It won't take but an instant." She took hold of Ryker's hand, pulled him forward across the counter, and kissed his cheek.

Ryker blushed a wild crimson color we could see from across the room. Chloé said to the customer, "Thank you. He's the best," and she came back to us.

I didn't need to ask permission to leave the sales floor; Faith waved us toward the elevator.

On the 7th floor, Nana became a three-star general in charge of us all. Apparently my mother had a system: she surveyed the choices, picked four, asked Chloé to select one, then handed Chloé's favorite and her own favorite to me to give to Joey Pierson, the salesperson, who was more than happy to let Nana dictate the shopping.

Cary offered his opinion in the bedding department that duvet covers were too hard to put on, and Nana responded, "She's going to have a man living with her, Cary. He can manage the hard work."

"I'm just saying," Cary said, but he kept quiet after that.

"Maybe he's right, Nana," Chloé said. "George isn't much of a house-chore kind of guy."

I should have followed Cary's example, but I couldn't keep quiet. The best I could do was avoid asking if George was going to pay rent, now that she owned an apartment. Instead I said, "Isn't it lucky that he hasn't moved in with you yet? I mean, so he doesn't have to move twice."

A scene flashed before me: Cary, Chloé with George, and my mother, filling up the three apartments on the 16th floor at West End Avenue at 98th Street. I wouldn't have to climb those damn stairs up to the 3rd floor of Chloé's brownstone ever again, but I felt excluded from the new enclave.

Then I came back to the present, "I'll help with your move anytime I'm not working. When do you think you'll transfer your things to the new apartment?"

"The last day of the month," Nana said.

"My landlord agreed that I could leave on short notice, as long as I cleaned the apartment," Chloé said.

Cary huffed, "Of course he agreed. He'll be able to raise the rent."

Nana tapped me on the arm, "Bergdorf's will be able to deliver everything tomorrow, right, Andy? I want things in place before she moves."

If my mother wanted it, I'd have to make sure it got done. I nodded in agreement, but she was already flipping through towels and didn't notice.

The purchases continued: vanity mirror, bathmats, dish towels, wastebaskets and ceramic tissue box cover – why a tissue box cover? I didn't understand. Sheets, blankets, silverware, planter pots, and on and on.

Nana patted Chloé's shoulder while I was signing the credit slip for the mound of merchandise, "Don't worry, darling. The furniture company said the couch and mattress will arrive before moving day. It's easier to get new ones than it is to move your old ones."

"I'm not worried, Nana. I'm overwhelmed."

"The curtains in the apartment will do for now, but you'll need to find a rug for the living room, and maybe a floor lamp."

"Cary, Nana, this seems like too much. It's wonderful, but…"

Cary interrupted, "This is what grandparents are for, sweetie. You're making Nanette and me happy, letting us do this."

I could see he was right. Both of them were radiant with pleasure. Joey Pierson was radiant too, seeing the total on the sales slip, even with my discount.

§§

Ponytail looked different. Maybe he'd had a haircut? Who could tell with it gathered back in a rubber band? He was reading something on his tablet, studying it, and tapping his nails on his desk.

"So, Mr. Brown," he said and went no further.

I waited.

He waited.

I blinked first. "Is everything okay?" I asked.

He lobbed back with a question, "How did you get here this morning?"

I didn't want to give him the satisfaction of saying what he wanted to hear. Usually I'm quick on the uptake for clever comebacks and diversions, but I couldn't think of anything except the truth. I waited as long as I could before I said, "I walked."

He rubbed his chin like he was considering a job change. Then he spoke, "You did something differently this week. What?"

I looked at him. I'd had my fill of appointments with this guy. I'd made it a point to be civil and nothing more. I had never pronounced his name out loud, and still he acted like he was in charge. "Why? What do you mean, something different?" I asked.

He scratched his left ear with his right hand. "Your weight loss has been consistent since our meetings began.

169

Weight isn't the whole story with heart health, but in your case, it is a primary barometer. Today, you weigh 210 pounds, exactly the same as last week."

I shrugged. The ass would never be satisfied. Did he applaud me for the 50 pounds that had evaporated from my body? No. Did he tell me I was a good patient? No. Instead, he was riding my tail about no change in seven days. Only seven days. I should go on an eating binge just to show him. Hot fudge sundaes, fried chicken with gravy and buttered biscuits, red meat.

He asked again, "So what was different?"

He sat silently, one hand on his desk, the other massaging his forehead.

His eyebrows jumped up and he said, "Oh, did you forget to tell a secret this week?"

His stupid secrets had nothing to do with me losing weight. Yes, it seemed I had been revealing certain things that I had kept to myself, but not because I was telling secrets, just because they blurted themselves into a conversation here and there.

I did a quick review of the previous week and couldn't remember anything I'd accidentally let slip. It had been a busy week at work, and then the news of Cary and Nana giving Chloé the apartment next to theirs, well, I'd been preoccupied all week.

Ponytail took my silence as an affirmative answer, and he smiled. I could have strangled him for that smile.

"So, please, Mr. Brown, please begin telling secrets again," he said.

At least he said "please."

He went on, "Is there anything in particular that you'd like to tell me? Anything that's been on your mind?"

What? He wanted me to talk about my love life? My finances? Not!

He must have heard my thoughts, because he tacked on, "About your health, I mean."

I started tapping my nails on the arm of the chair. Was I unconsciously mimicking what Ponytail had done earlier on his desk? I stopped tapping.

I chuckled as if I was going to tell a joke. "If I have another heart attack, I hope it's at work or at a party or while I'm eating at a restaurant."

Ponytail didn't laugh. Instead he cocked his head to the side, squinted at me, and asked, "Why's that, Mr. Brown?"

It sounded like he really wanted to know.

"Last time, I was at work, and I didn't have to do a thing. I didn't even know what happened, didn't feel anything. Everyone else took care of everything, and I woke up in a hospital. It was easy." I chuckled again.

"Easy?" he repeated.

"Well, yes, relatively speaking. I mean…," I searched around for words, "I mean, you know, if I'd been at home, alone, I could have lain there for hours, for days, without anyone noticing. I could have died and no one would have known."

He looked me directly in the eyes. "You haven't mentioned this to anyone, have you?"

"Uh… no," I said quietly.

"It worries you? That it might happen at home when you're alone?"

I didn't want to answer. Life on life's terms, and all that. Besides, what would it matter? I wouldn't know about it if I were dead.

I nodded Yes.

"That's a very logical worry, Mr. Brown," Ponytail said, still looking at me. "Let me tell you how you're doing since your heart attack occurred. It's not just your weight that has changed. Your LDL cholesterol was 167 when you were admitted to the hospital. Now," he looked at the tablet open on his desk, "it's 89. That's a very significant improvement. Your HDL cholesterol is 43, also very good."

I stared at him.

"Cholesterol is a primary indicator of arterial health," he said, like he was explaining to a 5th grader instead of to me, an experienced and intelligent man.

I didn't argue and kept listening.

"Your triglyceride level, another potential warning signal for heart attack, it's 132 md/dl, a drop of 32 points. That's milligrams per deciliter."

I sat forward. "Is that good?"

He smiled. It was a smile without irony. I'd bet he used a whitening gel.

"It's very good," he replied. "Besides that, your C-reactive protein level is low; that's good. You have low ceramides, much lower than in the first weeks after the

172

stents; that's good. You're not diabetic; also good." He glanced down again and went on, "And I ran the test for troponin T. That's a protein that can indicate heart disease risk, and yours is in the normal range."

Ponytail looked up from the screen. "In other words, what we've been doing...," he paused. I thought he was going to smile again, but I was wrong. "...what *you've* been doing has been very effective. If you can identify what has changed in your life since the heart attack, and if you continue doing those things, your chance for another heart attack is significantly reduced.

Changes? I'd been walking to work, and yes, I'd been telling things about myself now and again. But otherwise? Was I eating less? Not really. Maybe I was more aware of what I ate and whether I was hungry or not. But not enough to say my food habits had changed.

"I repeat," Ponytail said, "I want you to review this past week, and please, return to the routines you developed after your heart attack. I don't want your health to backslide."

I took a deep breath and looked at my hands in my lap. Maybe the guy wasn't such a jerk.

"I'm glad you told me about the worry of a heart attack when you are home alone," he said.

I wondered if I could count that as my week's secret.

"I'm going to write a prescription for you." He jotted something on his script pad and handed it to me. "It's

173

a gizmo to attach to a bracelet or necklace to press if you have a medical emergency."

Oh my god, I felt like a decrepit old man with a medic alert sign written on my forehead.

Ponytail was still talking: "It's tiny. No one will notice it, but it alerts the nearest fire department if it's pushed, and it's very effective. Wear it 24/7, and I hope you never need it."

He stood up and reached his arm toward me across his desk with his hand out.

I looked at the hand, and suddenly realized he was offering a handshake. That was a first. A weird first, as far as I was concerned. But I stood and took his hand, giving it a manly jerk, and said, "Thank you." Thank you? Why had I said that?

"I'll see you next week," he said, and he took his hand back.

I stumbled out of the office and walked toward Central Park South to go to work, replaying the entire session in my mind.

§§

It was the last day of the month. My alarm had gone off two hours earlier than normal so I could show up at 8 a.m. for my daughter's marathon move.

I was huffing when I walked into Chloé's apartment, "I'm glad the move goes downstairs here, and upstairs there with an elevator," I said. "I brought bagels from Barney Greengrass, and I hope someone has made coffee."

"Hi Daddy," Chloé replied. She was wearing sweatpants and a navy pullover that made her red glasses seem patriotic. "Cary brought Krispy Kreme donuts and I have bananas." She threw her hands in the air and called out happily, "I'm moving into my very own apartment! Yippee!"

George came from the direction of the kitchen carrying two grey mugs, and reached one out toward me.

The odor of fresh brewed coffee filled my soul. "Ah George, you're a better man than I ever imagined. Thank you."

"So what's first?" Nana asked from her perch on a step ladder.

"You're not in charge?" I mocked, and got a glare in return.

Chloé had a banana in one hand and picked up a notepad from the lamp table with the other. "I've put blue post-its on everything that's going to stay in the apartment. The Salvation Army will come this afternoon to clear out the place." She looked around to make sure we were nodding in agreement. "Yellow post-its are on boxes to go out on our first relay to 98th Street. Red post-its are for the second run."

"I told her red should be for stop, don't take it; green for let's go first; yellow for second, but she didn't listen."

Cary laughed, "You've made me forget the original system, George."

He smiled wryly, as if that had been his goal.

"I repeat," Chloé said, ignoring George, "Blue stays; Yellow out first; Red last."

"What's the difference between first and last?" I asked. "First goes in the refrigerator?"

A look of horror crossed Chloé face.

"You forgot about things in the fridge?" Nana asked. "Don't worry, I'll box those things up and they can go whenever I'm finished."

Chloé gave a sigh of relief and took the last bite of her banana. "Thanks, Nana. Just so you know, yellow-tag things are heavy, like boxed books, cleaning products, and furniture. Red signifies the lighter things, for when we're tired."

"The logic of an expert physio-therapist," Cary said. He slapped his knee and exclaimed, "So let's get started."

"My buddy's pick-up is double-parked just outside," George said.

Chloé lifted a rocking chair and headed to the open door. "Thank goodness for a sunny day."

I did my fair share of toting and never felt like my heart was in danger, although there were three boxes I tried to lift and backed away from. Probably medical books, I decided: perfect for muscular George to haul down the three flights of stairs.

Every time I re-mounted the stairs, I ate a few bites of bagel with cream cheese and drank some coffee to fortify myself for the next trip down. Five trips turned out to be sufficient for me and yellow post-its.

Cary stood in the middle of the living room and turned in a slow circle, nodding approval. "Not bad. The pick-up is full and the apartment is half empty."

We'd all heard stories of moving days gone bad with thieves absconding with full boxes, so Nana stayed in the apartment as guardian. Chloé and George took the truck; Cary and I went uptown on the bus.

At West End, we did a shuttle: Chloé and Cary unloaded and put things in the service elevator. With Blue as our supervisor, George and I met the elevator on the 16th floor and took Chloé's possessions into apartment 16C.

Finally, the two-bedroom apartment was full of yellow post-it boxes and furniture, and I was sweating. We locked up the new apartment, returned Blue to Nana's apartment, and rode down to the lobby, where I asked, "Can I ride in the truck going back to 87th Street?"

"Absolutely," Chloé answered. "We'll all fit," she said to Cary and me. "I'll ride in the back."

George ferried us to the old apartment. Nana was waiting for us on the stoop, and as we unfolded ourselves from the truck, she said, "Sit next to me in the sun here on the steps." She pulled tall glasses full of ice from a basket and filled them with yellow liquid. "I thought it was a better choice to eat the things in the freezer and fridge than to transport them. Here's lemonade."

I drained the glass and got a refill. Likewise with the others. Nana pulled out sandwiches and passed them around. "Eat whatever you get," she said. "No complaining."

Mine was thick roast beef with some kind of smelly cheese and mustard. I ate instead of criticizing.

"What do you have?" I asked Cary.

He cut his eyes toward Nana and said softly, "I think it's cut up hotdogs with Caesar salad." He swallowed. "Not too bad."

"My houmous and tomato is delicious, Nana," Chloé said. "I didn't realize how hungry I was."

"I saved the best for myself," Nana said, "Pastrami and corned beef with pickles and mayonnaise. How do you like yours, George?"

He was chewing and couldn't answer, but he nodded slowly.

Nana smiled, "I think he got the avocado and egg," which seemed to please us all. "No rush, but when you're finished, we still have donuts upstairs. Were all the

178

Bergdorf deliveries at the new apartment?" Nana asked. "The doorman promised me that he'd take the transport men up and watch them until they left."

"He did his job well," I said. "BG boxes were piled in the kitchen."

"The bed was there too, set up and ready for sheets and pillows," George said.

"George tried out the mattress and almost fell asleep," I said, "but to get him up, I rang the doorbell, which, by the way, works very well."

George rubbed his shoulder against Chloé's and said in a stage whisper, "The mattress is great, whenever you're willing to have sex again." He leaned in closer and added, "I hope it's soon." He winked, "And I promise from now on to wear protection."

I didn't want to hear about him and his intimate life with my daughter. He was smiling, and I wanted to punch him in the teeth, but I stayed sane and silent.

Nana, on the other hand, said what I was thinking: "You let her heal as long as she needs after her ordeal, George Kuykendall! Don't be pushing her until the bleeding stops completely."

Hooray for Nana.

George didn't answer her. He didn't even look afraid, like I would've been. Instead, he drained his glass and said, "You guys bring the red post-its down. I'll go to my apartment and load up the truck with my stuff. Everything there is ready. It'll take me a ½ hour, and I'll be back."

179

The rest of us trudged upstairs, and I silently thanked the gods that, soon, I'd never have to climb Chloe's damned steps again.

Inside the half-empty apartment, Nana hugged Chloé. "Is it hard to leave your home here? Do you think you'll be happy in the new apartment?"

"Oh Nana, I haven't spent one night in the new apartment, and I'm already happy there." She pulled Cary over and said, "Cary, the apartment is the most amazing gift I could have dreamed of. Next to you, in a beautiful building, with an extra bedroom and a snazzy modern kitchen, I'm in love with it. I'll never be able to thank you enough."

Cary ducked his head bashfully. "No need to thank me, my dear. You deserve that and more. You deserve the entire world."

Chloé pulled her grandparents close in a group hug. I watched and tried not to feel jealous or left-out. I hadn't been able to provide my daughter with an apartment of her own, but I wanted to be glad that she had Nana and Cary to help her.

Cary had always been around, it seemed like, almost 40 years since he and my mother had "been together" in separate apartments next to each other.

I'd lived in Nana's apartment until I graduated from Fordham. After graduation, Mom – she was still Mom to me back then, before my own child tagged her "Nana" – Mom had helped me find my first apartment to rent, on West 105th Street, a big studio in a building with a tiny elevator, and she had paid my security deposit and first month's rent. She and Cary helped me carry my clothes to the new place and gave me a bottle of champagne as a gift.

Immediately, my childhood bedroom had become Nana's storage space for finished paintings and blank canvases.

Me, I found out my girlfriend was pregnant, found a new job with Bergdorf Goodman, and then found an apartment to buy. A decade and a half later, when I divorced, my life didn't change much.

Maybe I would be able to do something extravagant for Chloé's children 20 or 30 years down the road. Not for the child who wasn't, but maybe there would be others. The new apartment had space for a baby or two.

"What are you planning for the second bedroom?" I asked, trying to keep a neutral expression so I didn't convey the picture of a nursery I had in my head.

Chloé laughed her lilting titter. "George tried to claim it as his office, but I put my foot down," and she stomped. "It's my office first, for my research, a quiet space. I told him if he can keep the noise down, then it can be his office too."

"He'll have to start using earphones and Bluetooth with all his clients," Cary said.

Chloé snickered, "Yes, well, we'll see."

"Are you ready?" Nana asked. "I can start down with the first armful of red-tagged things."

Chloé picked up a big box and handed it to her grandmother.

181

"What do you have in here?" Nana crowed. "Pigeon feathers?"

Chloé smiled, "Almost. The bed pillows and two comforters."

"That should have been my box," I whined with a smile.

"They're all like that," Chloé said. "Take your pick."

She was right. I carried down two large boxes at once as if I were Superman. Towels and t-shirts, I imagined. Or down jackets.

Nana stayed on the sidewalk with the first boxes while the three of us re-mounted for more. In less than an hour, we cleared the last of the red post-its, just in time to see George arrive in the pick-up.

When the truck was full, Chloé looked at her cell phone. "The Salvation Army should be here soon to pick up the blue post-its."

Nana didn't wait for instructions. "I'll wait here for them and let you do the work at West End."

Cary hugged her, "That's my love, always putting first dibs on the easiest job."

She pushed him away with a smirk. "When you get there, take Blue for a walk. I'll be here cleaning the old apartment so Chloé can get her deposit back."

"I'll come back and help," Chloé said.

"Oh, darling, stay in your new home and relax. I'll lock up and be there as soon as this place is empty."

Cary kissed Nana's cheek, "We'll order in for dinner. It will be waiting when you arrive."

"Come on, Daddy. You and I can take the bus. Cary, George will chauffeur you to 98th Street."

George flexed his biceps, smiling, "Yes. The *real* men will unload while we wait for you to arrive."

Chloé took my arm, and we walked away. "He wanted private time with Cary to thank him for the apartment. He knows it's in my name, but it is quite an upgrade for him. He really appreciates the new place."

I took a breath and patted Chloé's hand on my arm. "As long as you're happy, I'm happy," I said.

Maybe I was wrong about George. After all, I was prejudiced. My daughter was the smartest, prettiest young woman in the world. She had an upright character; she was good humored; she was funny; and she deserved someone as extraordinary as she was. Could that be the work-from-home voice-over agent, George Kuykendall? He was nice-looking and clean, but he seemed very ordinary to me. Then again, what did I know about love?

By the time, Chloé and I arrived, George had already left to return the pick-up to his friend, and all the red post-its were on the ground floor next to the service elevator with Cary standing guard.

"Three trips up," he predicted, and we stacked as many of the light boxes as possible in the elevator. At the 16th floor, we left Chloé to shuttle things into the apartment while Cary and I went down for more.

She and Blue met us when we arrived on her floor for the second time. "Just a few things left," I told her.

"Hold the elevator. I'll get Blue's leash and go down with you," Cary said.

Chloé was sliding boxes into the apartment when we descended.

"How old is Blue now?" I asked to fill the silence during the 16-floor descent.

"Almost 7 years old. My god, time passes fast." He watched the numbers of the floors going by. "I love this new leash. Chloe's still waiting for the patent to come through."

I smiled. It was always something with Chloé, an invention, an idea, a solution to a problem, or an analysis for a new approach. The dog leash idea had come to her when one of her patients was recuperating from a rotator cuff tear of the right shoulder.

Chloé had the guy use an elastic exercise band to rebuild his arm strength. It had 7 inch sections partitioned off so he could vary the resistance and distance of his exercise work.

The guy didn't have a dog, but Chloé had the inspiration that walking Blue would be easier for her grandmother with an elastic leash, one with high level resistance, flexible in its length with notched off sections, so there would be less joint stress when the dog pulled.

She made up a prototype, got various permissions, found a patent lawyer, and filled out various forms. The patent was still pending, but Four Paws Inc in New Jersey was already manufacturing and selling her leashes.

"Your granddaughter is an amazing person," I told Cary at the lobby.

"And your daughter is exceptionally talented," he replied with a smile, taking Blue outside for a walk.

I ferried up the last boxes and asked Chloé for a drink.

She paused her organizing and said, "Of course, Daddy. Let's see, I have tap water, and ah, tap water. Only I don't know where the glasses are."

I decided against drinking from the faucet. "You're a fabulous hostess, sweet girl." She accepted my sarcasm gracefully, and I said, "Let's sit on your new couch and order dinner. What sounds good to you?"

"Italian?"

"Vietnamese?" I suggested.

Another voice said, "Mexican." George was standing at the front door.

Chloé looked at me, and I nodded agreement.

"Mexican it is," she said.

George took over the chore of ordering, and before he was finished, Nana walked in with Cary and Blue. She handed a keychain to Chloé. "You are officially finished with the walk-up apartment on 87th Street."

Chloé jumped up and danced, singing, "Moving on up!" Clearly, she didn't know the words after the first few lines, but it did not diminish her enthusiasm.

185

Cary leaned over and whispered to me, "That's jumpstyle dancing."

I looked at him to make sure I'd understood him.

He nodded and added, "It's the new thing. I saw a class doing it at the gym the other morning."

She was still jumping when the doorbell rang. Blue barked, and George spoke at the intercom. "Food's on its way up," he announced.

Cary stood up and reached in his jeans back pocket for his wallet.

"Oh no," George said and pointed a threatening finger toward Cary. "It's my treat."

"Five people," I warned. "It'll kill a week's worth of your budget."

"He ordered, so he pays," Chloé said. "Besides, this way, you can blame George if you don't like the food."

George opened the door of the new apartment just as the delivery person got off the elevator. He handed the sacks to Chloé and paid.

I announced the items as she lifted containers out of the first bag and spread them on the new table at the edge of the living room: "Three orders of nachos with guacamole and three orders of chicken taquitos."

"Appetizers to share," George said, opening the next sac. "Tacos," he announced, pulling out six packages.

I peeked in each taco container to verify: "Fish, rice/corn/beans, pork, chicken, steak, and…" I paused to make sure I had it right, "…and pork with pineapple." I tipped an imaginary hat to George. "Four tacos in each flavor, plus chips, chips, chips and salsa."

There was a sack of Corona beers, and another with paper plates, plastic forks, and napkins.

My mouth was watering as I put taquitos on a plate and prepared to take my share of nachos, when Nana spoke up: "Where are the Margaritas? The caramel flan? The churros?"

"I won't have room for flan," I said, wiping sauce from my lips with the back of my hand. "The guacamole is great."

"This is perfect," Cary said while he took another bite of a steak taco.

Chloé patted George's knee and said, "It's delicious. Thanks." She had finished a chicken taco and was half-way into one with pork and pineapple.

"We should have a housewarming party," Nana crooned.

"Yeah," George jumped in. "Tomorrow?"

"Don't you need to unpack a few things first?" I said.

"Killjoy," Nana threw back at me.

"It has to be before you two go to Block Island," Chloé said.

I'd forgotten that Nana and Cary were going on vacation.

Chloé looked around at the mess in the apartment. "I can have enough of my things unpacked by Monday," she said.

"So Monday night," George announced.

"Or Tuesday," Cary inserted, "if you feel pressured or rushed."

Nana stood up and excused herself, saying, "I'll be right back."

In two minutes, she re-entered carrying a picture frame with its back toward us. "Before all your friends arrive for a party, I want you to have your housewarming present." She turned the painting around.

It was a swooping branch edged with big colorful flowers and leaves.

Chloé came up close to the piece and rubbed her hand gently over its textured textile surface. "Oh Nana. It's a Cristine Rodriguez! And so beautiful."

"I know you love her work," Nana said. "Enjoy it forever."

Chloé moved in close, so Nana had to set the edge of the frame on her feet to receive the hug. "It's wonderful. Thank you so much," Chloé murmured without stopping the hug.

I didn't know Rodriguez. But I liked the painting, if I could call it "a painting" since there wasn't any paint. I made a mental note that I had to find a house-warming gift too.

Half-way to Mount Sinai Hospital, I glanced over my shoulder to see if anyone on the sidewalk was watching me, and then I cinched my new Magnanni belt one hole tighter. My body was getting more and more bizarre; I barely knew it any longer.

In Ponytail's office, the scales clocked me in at 206 pounds. The last time I had weighed 206, I'd been … what? 18 years old? Ah, the good old days at Fordham University. I was living at home, but it was a life without rules, without hassle, full of self-righteous world-changing ideas and actions. It was a damn long time ago.

"I'm glad to see you're back on track with the weight loss, Mr. Brown," Ponytail told me. "Your blood pressure is good too."

I wanted to tell him he could call me "Andy." After all, he was in my datebook as often as my daughter or mother. But I stopped myself, and instead I said, "If I lose more weight, I'll have to get new clothes again."

His eyes twinkled. "Yes. You'll look stylish while you live a long time. On that note…" he paused, then went on, "your daughter is a physical therapist, isn't she?"

I nodded, not getting the connection.

"She will be able to give you exercises to build muscle mass which will reduce your sense of having too much skin after such dramatic weight loss."

So, it was evident at least to Ponytail that I had loose skin hanging everywhere. Probably everyone noticed it. I wasn't sure I wanted to talk about this to Ponytail. Was my physical appearance part of a nurse practitioner's domain?

I must have looked uncomfortable, because he added, "Or she could recommend someone else if you'd be more at ease with a stranger."

I didn't know what to say.

"I mention this only because some patients immediately look for surgery to correct the loose skin, but in your 50's your natural skin elasticity can adjust to the weight loss with time and exercise."

Once again, I hated Ponytail. But I had to ask, "Do I look terrible?"

This time the twinkle in his eyes made it to his lips, and one side of his mouth curved up. "You want my honest opinion or my medical opinion?"

I chewed on the question. "Your honest opinion," I answered.

"I think you look 15 years younger than when I met you, and with the sagging skin, you look 3 or 4 years older than you actually are. In other words, you are a handsome man now, whereas before, you were a fat man."

I pulled my chin back and shook my head. "Shit, you can do honest, I'll say that for you." I looked at him sideways, "And your medical opinion?"

"Yours is one of the most remarkable transformations I have seen during my career. I am proud to be part of your medical team. You look great, and I think you will live a long time, barring a bus running you down on Madison Avenue."

Was the bus line a joke? Was Mr. No-nonsense Ponytail being comical? I chuckled, thinking No…he wasn't funny; he was just covering his ass in case I died next week.

He stood up and reached his hand out. This time, I knew it meant he was offering a handshake. Something had shifted between us, and I didn't know what it was.

"See you next week," he said as we locked hands.

I murmured "Yes" and left.

§§

I drummed my fingertips on the counter, wondering what Chloé would like for a house-warming gift. I reviewed the floors at Bergdorf Goodman: a year's worth of haircuts? 20 free meals at the restaurant? A new swimsuit and a long weekend at Martha's Vineyard? A gift certificate for shoes? Maybe a fur coat…no, no dead animals. And no high-end designer clothes, where a month's salary equaled one dress, not for Chloé. Jewelry? A handbag?

Nothing clicked. Of course, I could always give her perfume.

"Excuse me, sir."

The voice jerked me out of my thoughts.

"Oh! No, excuse *me*, madam. I was … well, it doesn't matter why I was lost in my thoughts. I am here now, for you. You have my complete attention."

She was not a customer I knew. 30-ish, sporty, with boyishly short brown hair. "I'm looking for a gift," she said, and with a sly grin, she added, "I always find what I want, and end up buying two, the second one for myself. But I have a budget."

I liked her immediately: someone who didn't take herself seriously. "May I ask the budget?"

She sighed and said, "$35 for her. Times two if you include me."

Her sigh was well placed. $35 didn't go far, not here at Bergdorf Goodman or anywhere else. We didn't have sales in the perfume department. But I refused to be negative with a client I liked, and I was never stumped. I crossed my arms, rested my chin in one palm, and looked around my area. "What does your friend do for fun?" I asked. "How old is she?"

The brunette stood up straight, like she had joined my quest. "She's my age. That's 33. Single. A working mother."

"What kind of work?"

She laughed, "She's a film archivist for the Wildlife Conservancy at the Bronx Zoo. Whoever heard of such a job?"

"What do you do?" I asked. She looked startled, and I added, "Not to be personal, but I am actually looking for a gift for you, right? Not just your friend?"

She nodded and relaxed. "Oddly enough, I'm an animal person too. I raise funds for Guide Dogs for the Blind. Neither one of us touch animals every day, not like a veterinarian, but animals are the focus of our work."

"So, you don't want to have a smell that's offensive to animals." I cringed and said, "That didn't come out right."

She laughed again. "I understand. And you're right. What can you suggest?"

I had an idea, but I started with something else. I found a handful of testers for Nest New York fragrances. "These come in cute roll-on bottles, and they smell great;

Wild Poppy, Dahlia, Citrine, Wisteria." She sniffed each fragrance, and I announced, "$28 each. We're in the budget."

She nodded. "They're cute, conveniently small. Yes. Anything else?"

"Follow me," I said and led her to the Kiehl's counter. "This is a line that has been around for more than 170 years, developed in New York City." I glanced over my shoulder to see if anyone was listening. Karen Jacobs, the Kiehl's sales manager knew me and left us alone. "In my opinion, it's the best skin care. The best." I made a gesture that indicated no other words were necessary. "I use it myself. And my daughter too. She's just a few years younger than you and your friend."

I pulled the tester for the Crème de Corps over and let her pump some in her palm. "It's not fancy, but it's the best."

She rubbed her hands together and sniffed. "Humm," she commented.

"Here's the Crème de Corps Dry Body Oil," I said and pumped a drop onto the back of her hand.

"Oh, that's nice," she reacted. She looked up at me. "Kiehl's is expensive?"

I wiggled my eyebrows and answered, "It's reasonable. The oil is $18 and the lotion is $14."

Her face lit up. "So I could get both for her. And for me too."

I nodded.

"Well, it has to be Kiehl's. I mean, perfume is nice, but we'll actually use these products."

So, I had been right. She was a West Side woman, pretty and practical, instead of an East Side princess. Those were terrible Manhattan stereotypes, but in this case, they had guided me well.

"Shall I have yours gift-wrapped as well as your friend's?"

She smiled. "Neither one. I like wrapping presents."

I walked back to the perfume counter carrying her products. "I bet you tie a wonderful gift bow," I told her.

After I had rung up the sale and handed her the BG bag, I gave her my card and said, "Come back anytime, Ms. Barber."

She had half-turned to leave when she stopped and asked me, "What were you thinking about so hard when I walked up?"

I felt my face go hot. "I'm usually very present in my work." She waited, so I went on. "My daughter, the one I mentioned, she just got a new apartment, and I was trying to decide on a house-warming present."

She winked at me and held up her BG bag. "You'll find the perfect gift for her too, I'm sure."

The client was always right, as they say. I just needed to ask the right questions about Chloé. I knew her, who she was, what was important to her, how she entertained herself. I looked around the perfume department and immediately knew this was not where I would find her gift.

§§

Blue and Nana greeted the next surge of guests at the door of the new apartment.

"All three doors on this floor are open. We didn't know where the party was," Nicole Fisher said.

Nana and Nicole exchanged kisses on both cheeks. "Oh, I'm so glad everyone could come on such short notice," Nana said. She greeted Nicole Fisher and her friends from the apartment building on Central Park West. "This is the housewarming site, but the party is in all three apartments. You know my apartment next door, and Cary's. Now, come in and see Chloé's new place."

George stood next to me at Chloé's bookcase and asked, "Are you sure you can deal with a Bose? The SoundDock is sort of modern, you know."

"I'm not old yet, George. I know how to play music. And a party needs music."

He looked me directly in the eyes, but it felt like he was peering down his nose at me. "I don't think it's a dancing kind of party, Andy."

I didn't bother to smile. "Go be with your guests, George. I'll be fine here." He had barely turned his back when I revved up my play list with Boney M doing *Sunny,* Stan Getz with *Night and Day*, and Ben Webster's *Stormy Weather*." It was going to be a great night.

All of George's friends were strangers to me, and they all looked alike: 30-ish, blue jeans, men with a tie, women with a see-through blouse.

Chloé's long-time friends came up to me when they arrived: "Hi, Mr. Brown," "What a great place Chloé has now!" "She helped me so much last year," "She told me the apartment was wonderful, but I didn't expect this," "You look great, Mr. Brown. What've you been doing?" "I promise I won't drink as much as I did at Chloé's birthday two years ago," "Long time no see, Mr. Brown." And on and on. I didn't remember most of their names, but their faces and attitudes were part of the scenery of my daughter's life.

The guests circulated through the three apartments holding glasses and small blue paper plates full of cupcakes or shrimp, boiled eggs stuffed with salmon or apricot bruschetta, guacamole or pigs-in-the-blanket, or one of the dozen other things Nana had ordered for the night.

Ryker and his partner Dave came up to me, with three wine glasses between the two of them. "I thought you might be able to use this," Ryker said, handing me one of the glasses.

Handsome Dave -- at least that's what I called him in my head, because he was 6 feet tall, impeccably groomed, with a tinge of grey at the temples of his lush black hair -- Handsome Dave scanned the room and said, "It's quite a crowd here."

"Yes, just an intimate gathering that stretches through three apartments," I sneered lightly. "Three generations of people making small talk."

Handsome Dave took a sip of his wine and said, "Yes, it's lovely that they mingle so easily."

"Frank Bryson from jewelry is here. And Karen Jacobs. Of course, Faith's somewhere around," Ryker told me. "Have you seen her?"

"Not yet."

"She brought Chloé a bottle of wine as a gift," Ryker said.

"She's not the only one. You should see the kitchen counter. We could set up bar for the Olympic Drinking Games."

"It'll all get used," Handsome Dave said. Then pointing toward the opposite wall, he added, "Ryker and I brought a potted lemon tree."

"Great idea," I said. "It's beautiful."

"It'll last longer than the liquor," Ryker laughed.

Cary came over with someone familiar. Oh yes, our benefactor from New York City Ballet. I found the name in my memory bank, "Hi, Ned," I said.

Cary gave me an approving glance because he knew how bad I was with names of people who weren't clients. He said, "The ballet is dark on Mondays, so Ned came with his entourage."

"I think half the orchestra is here," Ned laughed. "I promise, I didn't tell them it was free food and drinks."

"They're all welcome," I said, acting like a gracious host. "You're helping my daughter christen her new home. It's a great place, don't you think?"

He didn't respond. Instead he cocked an ear toward the bookshelf where my playlist was rolling through its selections. "Is that Ben Webster doing *Mack the Knife*? I love that guy." He turned around and called across the room, "Pete, come over here."

I couldn't forget that name: Paunchy Pete, the flute player. Shaped opposite to his instrument.

They started comparing saxophonists. I wanted to hear every word, but Cary pulled me aside, "I have a couple of banker friends here I want you to meet, Andy."

I excused myself and followed Cary to his apartment where an older crowd sat on the couch and chairs.

Blue was sitting at the feet of a woman in shiny purple slacks and a beige blazer. "Bernice, this is my step-son I was telling you about."

"No, no, please don't get up," I told her. Oh my god, was Cary trying to fix me up with a woman? Surely, he and Nana had figured out by now that I wasn't in the dating market.

Cary pulled a couple of chairs close. "You don't mind us joining you, do you, Bernice?"

"Not at all, Cary. It's always a pleasure to have time with you. Your apartment is as wonderful as you said."

He looked at me and explained, "I've been telling Bernice how lucky we are, Chloé, Nanette, and I, to be able

199

to live so close together, and how I wish you were here too." He turned back to Bernice, "Like I told you, Andy has a great apartment on 69th and Amsterdam, no mortgage, free and clear, but I'm on a mission to find another apartment in this building to buy."

The truth was, I had three more years to finish paying the mortgage on the apartment I'd bought when Tanya and I married. But with inflation, after 27 years, the payments were less than my electricity bill.

Purple-pants Bernice responded, "It's a fine idea, Cary. And you know I'll do whatever it takes to make it work for you."

"So Andy, I'm giving you notice," Cary said. "Whenever I find what I'm looking for, I'm going to twist your arm to move up to 98th Street to be with your family; clearly, the apartment won't be on the 16th floor, but I want you here. Your mother would never say this to you, but she needs you closer."

The first thing that came to my mind was how much longer the walk would be from 98th Street to Bergdorf's. I felt exhausted thinking about it.

Then I stared at Cary. Did he always talk about me as his step-son? I mean, I was almost grown when he came into Nana's life, and he never married her. Here in his home, the public announcement of his long-term connection between us touched me.

I hadn't mentioned to anyone that I'd felt left out of the 98th Street cozy-family thing. I had to admit, that had been a secret of mine. Whether I ever moved or not, Cary's

200

solicitude made me feel embraced in a way that was surprisingly comforting.

"To be included means a lot to me, Cary. We'll see," I said sincerely.

Purple-pants Bernice laughed, "We'll see? Andy, hold on tight, because in my experience, when Cary Lambert sets his mind on a project, the project gets done." She turned to Cary to say, "Nanette told me you're going on a vacation soon."

Cary nodded, "Yes, in a few days, to The Surf Hotel. Do you know it?"

"On Block Island? I've never been there but I hear it's excellent."

A man next to Bernice joined in to say, "I've always stayed at the National Hotel." The conversation veered off, and finally I excused myself to check on the music.

Heading back to Chloé's new home, I passed the open door of Nana's apartment and watched two middle-aged creative-types laugh at something George was saying. I hadn't imagined George as an artist entertainer, but there it was: proof that I could be wrong.

In the new apartment, Ella was singing *Something's Gotta Give*. At the Bose, the playlist looked like it was working without problems.

Nana tapped me on the shoulder. "A good turn-out for Chloé," she said.

I searched the living room for the spiked hair and red glasses. Chloé was leaning against a wall talking to three young men and a young woman. I couldn't tell from her body language if they were friends or former patients. "She looks happy, Nana. You and Cary did a good thing for her with this apartment."

"Unfortunately, I can't take the credit," she said. "It was all Cary. So, he gets to be right for once." She didn't smile, but her sarcasm was light-hearted.

"Andy! Ms. Brown!"

I hadn't seen Faith approach, but I recognized her high-pitched voice without looking. I saved Nana the awkward moment of not knowing the blond woman who had called out her name by responding, "Faith, I'm glad you could come. Ryker and Dave told me you brought Chloé a bottle of wine. But no Bergdorf crystal decanter?"

Without looking at me, Nana gave a subtle nod of understanding: Faith from Bergdorf's was greeting us.

Faith punched my shoulder playfully and chuckled, "Wine for this party; decanter for the next party. What a wonderful apartment! I'm sure your granddaughter is thrilled," she said to Nana.

"The best is having her happy," Nana replied. "Andy, refill Faith's glass." With a smile, she added, "If you'll excuse me, I see someone else at the door who has just arrived."

Ned Lewis walked up to me with two other NYCB people. "I bet Tommy that we're listening to Blues Delight. Tell me I'm right."

"How much did you bet?" I asked dryly.

"Twenty bucks."

"That's enough to buy me a hamburger for lunch," I replied. "You're right. It's *Slightly Hung Over* by Blues Delight." I watched the thin man pull out his wallet and pass a bill to Ned.

"You remember Skinny Tommy?" Ned asked.

"Oh yes, the percussionist," I said.

The curly-haired woman next to him said, "I love the music that's playing."

Her name was on the tip of my tongue.

Faith chirped, "Andy's the one in charge of music. Hi. My name's Faith Reynolds. I work with Andy."

A flash came to me. I gestured toward the woman with curly hair and said to Faith, "This is Shannon Shriver; no relative to Maria, Eunice, or Sargent."

Shannon laughed, "Well. There's a good memory. It's your daughter who lives here. Right?"

Skinny Tommy smirked and said to me, "She's been drooling over the building and the apartment, as if she doesn't have a 2-bedroom of her own next to Zabar's Market."

Shannon hung her head, "Yes, but it's noisy there on Broadway. It's calm over here on West End."

"Andy," Ned said, "Twenty bucks that you don't remember what instrument Shannon plays."

Faith looked at me and asked, "Does this guy have a gambling problem?"

Tommy answered, "No. Ned talks. That's all."

Ned shrugged. "Chit chat with strangers is what I do for a living. I'll try anything different to stay out of the conversational rut. Sorry."

"Include dessert with the lunch you owe me, and I'll tell you Shannon's instrument."

"You're on," Ned said.

I felt a Cheshire cat smile covering my face. "Trumpet. Right, Shannon?"

She nodded. "I told you, Ned. The man's got a memory."

Ned nodded and said, "Let me know when you want to go to lunch."

"Sometime this month. Let's ask Cary to come along," I said.

Faith chirped, "I want to come too. Do you think Ryker will let us leave at the same time?"

Shannon gawked, "Well, if *you're* going, *I* want in on this lunch too."

Skinny Tommy spoke up, "I'm in. Where're we going?"

Ned groaned, "I shouldn't take them out in public. They're better locked up in the orchestra pit."

Chloé came up and said, "I just put out more snacks. This time, onion rings and cheese sticks. They're better when they're hot."

Faith gave Chloé a hug, saying, "I'm so excited for you here in the new place."

Shannon agreed, "It's a great apartment."

I did the introduction thing one more time: "Chloé, you remember Ned from the New York City Ballet? And Shannon and Tommy?"

"I'm glad you could make it. Yeah, I'm with you; it's a terrific apartment."

Ned talked to my daughter as if she were an old friend, "Chloé, I saw two of your grandmother's paintings here, but there was a third one on the wall over the couch, a woven piece. Was it a Cristina Rodriguez?"

Chloé's eyebrows shot up over her red frames. "So you know ballet and art both? Impressive," she replied. "Yes, that was my housewarming gift from Nana. I love it."

Tommy cringed, "And I only brought a box of chocolates."

"That's good too," Chloé said letting her tinkling laugh spread over the little group. "I adore chocolate."

I swallowed my embarrassment that the famous painting was better than what I had decided on, and put my arm over Chloé's shoulder. "This seems like a good time for me to give you *my* housewarming gift."

I pulled a Bergdorf Goodman bag off the bookshelf and handed it to her. "I thought about giving you a ticket to visit your mother in L.A." I enjoyed the panic that crossed her face and went on, "Then I switched to a new phone, or a computer, but finally, I decided on this."

She reached in the bag and pulled out a box the perfect size for a BG handkerchief, tied with a purple bow. She opened the box and saw the white tissue paper sealed with a BG sticker. I could tell she was confused. She had no idea what was inside, exactly as I had hoped.

She opened the tissue paper and saw the small envelope emblazoned with the insignia of the New York City Ballet. We were all watching, and I got the reaction I wanted when she opened the envelope.

"Yyyeeeeeeessss!" she squealed. "The Ballet!"

Immediately, she had her arms around me in a bear hug. "Thank you, Daddy. Thank you, thank you!"

"It's a season subscription for two, sweetheart. Enjoy."

It wasn't a gift in the same bracket as an Upper West Side apartment or a work of art, but I was pleased with the choice. Her grandmother had raised Chloé to love the arts. In fact, Nana had done the same for me, but with Chloé, it had stuck. Since she'd lived on her own, my daughter stuck to her budget, which meant she saw the occasional movie, but opera and ballet were rare.

"I've got to show George," she twittered, giving me another hug and running off.

"Good present. You did well," Faith said.

Ned was nodding. "I could have helped you with that, if you'd given me a call, Andy."

"You helped, Ned. You gave me the idea with our night at the ballet. She was so happy there; I thought I'd give her more happiness."

"All these gifts," Shannon said. "I need to throw a party for myself." She turned to me, "Will you come? I can give you my gift wish list."

I stammered, without any words coming out.

She leaned in so her shoulder touched mine, "I'm joking."

"But I hear she collects brass instruments," Skinny Tommy said with a straight face.

I was saved from having to come up with a witty response because George came in, pulling Chloé by the hand, with a trail of guests behind her.

"That's right," he called out. "Everyone has to come into our new home." He pulled Chloé close and kissed her cheek. "Yes, there's more to drink and eat," he laughed and continued talking to the crowd pushing in, "but before you party on, I want you here, because…" he paused dramatically, and turned Chloé around to face him, "because I am going to ask this lovely woman to marry me." He pulled a small box from his pocket, got down on one knee, opened the box to show a ring, and said, "Chloé Brown, will you spend the rest of your life with me?"

The room erupted into a cheering mass. Everyone was hugging the person closest. The party had gone crazy. I took a step back and felt my joy about the ballet tickets evaporate. Of course, my gift did not have to be the best thing in my daughter's life, but George had upstaged me to a monumental level, without giving Chloé even a few minutes to appreciate the NYCB subscription.

I moved my lips into a smile.

Chloé, on the other hand, was not smiling. Her eyes were the size of giant olives and her mouth was gaping like an old tennis shoe. George took the ring out of its box and slid it on her finger. He stood up, hugged her, and raised her hand in the air as if she were the winner in a boxing match. "We're going to be married!" he sang out.

Suddenly, Chloé was surrounded, with everyone congratulating her, kissing her, hugging her, toasting her. The happy buzz continued until George reached into the scrum, found Chloé hand, and took her away. Maybe he was taking her to Nana's apartment since it was bigger, so the crowd could celebrate more?

I stayed where I was in Chloé's new home, listening to Herbie Hancock play *Cantaloupe Island*.

§§

Nana and a few of her artist friends were in her apartment surrounded by paintings, but half the guests had left.

In the new apartment, my playlist had run its course, and George and Chloé relaxed in the living room with a few of their friends drinking beer.

Ryker and Handsome Dave, Faith, Cary, and I sipped wine in the new kitchen. My cell phone rang, and when I saw the caller ID, I stood up. Nobody noticed when I walked to the bathroom.

"Hi Tanya," I answered. "What's up?"

"Hello back at you," my ex-wife said. "I wanted to know where our daughter is registered for baby gifts. I thought it was better to ask you than her or Nanette."

Oh my god. Chloé had never called her mother with the baby update. I looked at my watch: late dinner time in L.A. The best choice was to tell Chloé to call her mother. Or for her mother to call her daughter directly. Whichever, Tanya was a few chapters behind the rest of us on her daughter's story.

"Where are you?" I asked.

"In my living room. Hal's in the viewing room, watching an old film. Or maybe it's an uncut unreleased film. I'm not sure. Anyway, it's a Monday night and we're both here. Though I'm not sure for how long."

209

That was a hook, if I'd ever heard one. Did I want to ask how her relationship with producer Hal Johnson was going? Yes. Did I want to listen to the answer? No.

"So you're not on the road with Matthew McConaughey." It wasn't a question.

"His new film is shooting here until next month. Then we're going to the Grand Canyon. It shouldn't interfere with my trip to New York. About the baby registry?"

I took a breath. "Are you sitting down?" That was a stupid thing to ask. It was as if talking to Tanya pushed me into insipid movie dialogue.

"Well, I am now. Do you have something to tell me?"

I was the one who needed to sit down. I sank onto the closed toilet seat, took a breath, and said, "Chloé has been meaning to call you, but I understand her delay. I'm sure she would rather do anything than go through it all again."

"What? Andy! What's happened? Is she okay? I can fly out tonight. Right now. I'm putting the phone down to get out my suitcase."

"Tanya. Tanya," I yelled into the telephone. I had royally screwed up this conversation. "TANYA!"

"What? Andy? Are you there? I can still catch the 10:48 flight if I hurry."

"Tanya, slow down. You don't have to come to New York. Chloé is fine."

I heard a sigh of relief the size of an avalanche. "Oh, you had me so scared. So our girl is okay? I'm so glad. And the baby? He's okay too? Or she."

"That's what Chloé wanted to tell you."

Tanya start to speak, and I interrupted firmly, "Tanya. Wait a minute. Let me tell you."

There was silence on the line.

"Thank you," I said. I decided to be blunt and save time. "A few weeks back, Chloé had an abortion."

The silence continued, until a small voice squeaked out, "Was there a problem with the fetus?"

I wished I were anywhere else other than in the bathroom during a party talking with my ex about our daughter. Yes, I understood Chloé avoiding a conversation about the abortion where she'd have to relive the details, and I hated replaying the loss for myself.

"It wasn't that. George and Chloé decided they weren't ready to have a baby."

I heard a mew, as if Tanya were a hurt kitten, and strangely enough, I knew how she felt.

"She…They…She's okay?" Tanya asked.

"She's fine. It was difficult, and she's fine."

I let Tanya take all the time she wanted. Me, I tried to distance myself from my reactions. "I hope you can realize why she was reluctant to call and talk about it."

The mew came through the receiver again. Then a sigh. "I've been a terrible mother. I should have been there with her. It's so hard to be pregnant. Why didn't she tell me what she was going to do?"

That was a question I was not going to answer. Instead I said, "Didn't you ever keep something from your parents when you were young? Something they wouldn't have easily accepted? I know I did, and I can't believe that you were more perfect that I was." I laughed at my own bad joke.

"You!" she scoffed. "You, with your famous mother and rich step-father, you never kept a secret in your life."

I kept on laughing. My ex would love the saga of my post-heart-attack treatments. "Ah Tanya, the stories I could tell you."

"I know enough stories. I don't want to know more," she growled. "So, tell me, is she still moving in with George?"

Chloé had warned me to keep my nose out of her business. If I remembered correctly, her words had been: "You don't respect me enough to do the *one* thing I ask." That one thing was to keep silent about the baby and her private life, especially with her mother.

I'd told too much of her story already, but I hadn't wanted Tanya to start shipping baby paraphernalia to New York City.

"I know Chloé would like to hear from you, Tanya. Maybe tomorrow when you've had a chance to…"

To what? To calm down? To cancel your plane reservation for the birth of the baby? To get the focus off of yourself and onto the tender feelings of your daughter?

"...to organize what you want to say, you can call her." That was simple. No mention of the new apartment from Cary and Nana, no mention of George's proposal of marriage.

Marriage. That was ironic. They could have gone ahead with the pregnancy and become a happy family of three. I groaned, then hoped Tanya hadn't heard me.

Another idea snuck into my mind: George wasn't willing to marry my daughter when he got her pregnant, but now that she owned a two-bedroom Upper West side apartment, he popped the question. Could Chloé's boyfriend be cagey enough to know that marriage was the easiest way for him to get his name on the deed of her property?

I stopped. I was tired, I'd had a few drinks, and I was making up fairy tales. "It's late here, Tanya. Let me know if your plans for coming here change."

She said something, and I hung up.

When I went back to the kitchen, Nana had arrived and was sitting next to Cary. I refilled my wine glass and sat down.

"Your friends left?" I asked her.

"No. They're jabbering on," she replied, then looked at me sideways. "You look different, Andy. You look good."

Did that mean I looked bad before? Apparently, she hadn't noticed I'd lost weight. So much for the insightful vision of a painter.

I said, "It's probably my new shirt. It's one of your colors."

She corrected me: "It's more peach than orange."

"So you're going on a vacation, I hear," Ryker said to her.

Nana smiled. "Yes, Wednesday, Cary and I are off to Block Island."

Faith gushed, "Someone told me that Block Island has 17 miles of beach. It sounds like paradise."

"You should come with us," Nana said. It was obvious she didn't mean it, but it was the kind of thing she said when she knew the answer ahead of time. Faith would never be able to get time off from Bergdorf on short notice.

"You're driving?" Handsome Dave asked.

"Nanette wanted to go by train, but my Audi needs an adventure, so it'll be a road trip."

"It's the first time you haven't had to share dog-walking duties with Chloé when we go out of town," Nana said to me. "Chloé and George are now the resident dog-sitters."

I kept a neutral face instead of yelping with the joy and relief I felt.

"I'll never forget that I was lucky enough to hear George propose marriage to your granddaughter," Faith swooned. "It was so romantic."

Nana nodded and said, "Yes, it turned out to quite an event." She sent me a glance that I couldn't interpret. Was she irritated that something happened at her party that she hadn't organized? Or was she ready to escape and get to bed?

Faith spoke to Nana in a loud, confidential whisper, "And that woman flirting with Andy! I've seen women put the moves on him at the store, but not up close and personal like this."

I didn't know what Faith was talking about. No one had flirted with me. "George's proposal must have ignited your imagination, Faith. There was no woman."

"Yes, that woman," Faith repeated, "the one with the curly hair, what was her name? The musician from Lincoln Center?"

"I met her," Nana said. "She came with Cary's friend from the gym, Ned. But I don't remember her name. So many people came, friends of friends, people I didn't know."

Faith snapped her fingers, "Shriver. Maria Shriver."

Ah, the light dawned on me. "You mean the trumpet player Shannon Shriver. No relation to Sargent, Maria, or Eunice. She wasn't flirting, Faith."

"Oh, yes, she was," Faith contradicted, as if we were at lunch in junior high talking about boy-girl crushes.

"Humm," Nana replied, staying non-committal. "Interesting." She didn't sound interested at all.

I switched the conversation back to reality, "Make sure Cary drives safely on the way to Block Island."

"Will you paint while you're there?" Ryker asked.

"No paints, no camera, just eating and relaxing," she said.

"It's their anniversary," I explained.

Nana touched Cary's arm. "I'm going to clear out everyone from my apartment." She yawned and stood up. "I doubt we'll see you before we leave, Andy." At the door with Cary, she added, "Watch after Chloé."

She didn't say the obvious: that George was watching after her granddaughter now, so I was superfluous.

"You've got such a nice mother, Andy," Faith said. "It must have been wonderful growing up with a mother like that.

I harrumphed, Handsome Dave laughed, but it was Ryker who replied, "Faith, outsiders never know what goes on inside a family."

"But she's so talented and she knows everyone," Faith argued. "Andy's proof that she was a good mother."

"She has been great with Chloé," I conceded. "I'll give her that much. With me…," I paused and shrugged, "she was my mother. What can I say?"

That made Ryker chuckle. "I understand, Andy. *Everyone* loves my mother, but growing up with her taught me how to lie. The less she knew how I passed my days, the safer I was."

"No, Ryker. That's not possible. When she came to Bergdorf's with you last week, she was charming. I loved her accent."

"When he lived with her, Faith, Ryker's mother didn't have an accent," Handsome Dave teased. "They both spoke German to each other."

Faith shooed off the comment with her hand.

Ryker sighed nostalgically, "I'd still be in trouble if Mutti knew how young I was the first time I had sex, or how often I slipped out at night to pick up my friends in the family car, or how I arranged for a smart friend to take my Abi test so I could get out of high school."

Faith looked horrified. "You didn't do those things!"

Ryker smiled. "Oh yes, I did. And lots of other things too."

"Which all helped you be the great man you are today," I laughed.

Handsome Dave took Ryker's hand and nodded agreement.

"Andy, I'm sure you hid things from your parents too," Ryker said.

"I certainly did," I answered. "On the outside, they were liberal. On the inside, they worried about appearances, and everything I wanted to do was out of bounds."

Faith leaned her elbows on the kitchen table and rested her chin on her palm. "Your mother seems so open and accepting."

I thought back through my life with my mother, before and after Dad died. Had I been afraid of Nana's disapproval? It didn't matter. She and I still talked, superficially, but we talked, even after decades of our strong personalities butting up against each other.

I asked Faith, "Do you remember back in the 1980's when AIDS was spreading and ACT UP started its political demonstrations?"

Faith nodded. She was a native New Yorker, like me. There was no way she could have missed the political upheavals of the city during those last decades of the 20th Century.

"I helped toss thousands of fake $100 bills from the Stock Market's balcony onto the trading floor during the ACT UP rally. We were all arrested."

"ACT UP?" Ryker asked.

"AIDS Coalition to Unleash Power," I explained. "It sounds violent, doesn't it? In a way, it was. No guns, but we caused a lot of trouble. Four days later, the charges were dropped and big pharmaceuticals lowered the price of AIDS medications."

"That's brave, Andy. I bet your mother was proud of you," Faith said.

"She would have killed me. My arrest would have ruined her reputation as the happy artist-mother. Luckily, she never found out. I was 19, a sophomore in college, living at home right here in the apartment next door, and it was my friends who bailed me out. Nana still has no idea…," I gave Faith a stern stare, "… and don't you tell her!"

Faith rolled her eyes as if to say, "Who me?"

"Promise," I demanded.

She ducked her head and said, "I promise."

Ryker sniggered and said, "My mother still thinks I'm a practicing Catholic."

"Instead of a raving atheist like me," Handsome Dave laughed.

"I let her believe what she wants to keep the peace," Ryker said.

"Enough," I said. "We're all adults who can do as we please, and I'm heading home to go to sleep."

Handsome Dave was on his feet before me. "Yes, let's go," he said. "I've had too much wine."

Ryker nodded agreement.

Faith groaned and cranked herself out of her chair. "You think Chloé would let me sleep on her couch so I don't have to take the bus home?"

"Take the subway," Ryker said. "It's faster."

"The bus is safer," I argued.

We said quick good-byes to Chloé and the others in the living room, and went down the elevator, still arguing about Faith's trip home to Queens. On the sidewalk, instead of waiting for her choice between bus and subway, I caught a cab down to 69th Street.

We went through the ritual again: blood pressure and pulse, weight, thumping and listening to chest and back. He did another blood sample. Then Ponytail said, "Here's a questionnaire I'd like you to fill out." He slid some pages toward me. "Actually, not me. The hospital wants you to answer their questions. Me, I only have one question: how are you feeling?"

I was breathing, awake, doing the things I was supposed to do. That meant I was feeling okay. I shrugged and said, "I'm fine."

Ponytail nodded, without making a note of my answer. "I want you to feel young and enthusiastic. Do you?"

I didn't have to ruminate on it. "No," I said.

This time, his nodding seemed more sincere. "Let's suppose that is ½ because of your health and ½ because of your psychological state."

"Let's suppose it's because I'm 52 years old."

He smiled, like it was a joke I'd made. I'd seen Ponytail smile several times now.

"Do you cough a lot?" he asked.

"No."

"Do you have pain when you urinate?"

"No."

"Do you have skin rashes?"

"No."

He recorded everything I said.

"Any dizziness?"

"I thought you only had one question."

He looked up from his tablet. "Any dizziness?"

"No."

"I'm going to change your medication," he said. He wrote on a prescription pad. "For two weeks, take your Enalapril every second day. In other words, I halving the dosage. On the non-Enalapril days, take one Bisoprolol. If you feel dizziness or have headaches, stop taking it and call me."

I looked at him suspiciously. Why the change? Bisoprolol? My expression must have said what I was thinking.

"There's research in Denmark that says both Enalapril and Bisoprolol may increase good moods," Ponytail said. "The research is persuasive. If you're feeling 'fine' with Enalapril, maybe the Bisoprolol will help you feel 'better than fine.' Maybe not. Enalapril is an ace inhibitor; Bisoprolol is betablocker. They work in different ways, but both control your blood pressure."

Apparently, the guy did more that write down my weight. It seemed he read to stay up to date in his field. I was mildly impressed.

"When will I be able to stop taking drugs altogether?" I asked. "Not taking drugs would bring down my blood pressure and kick start my good mood too."

"You don't like taking medication?" he asked.

"Nobody likes taking pills," I scoffed.

Ponytail pressed his lips together. "Many people like taking pills," he said. "It's an emotional dependance. They take a pill and feel like someone is taking care of them, someone more powerful than themselves." He paused, then added, "Medication helps sick people too."

"With the stents, I'm not sick anymore, right?"

"Mr. Brown, you have heart disease. We need to keep your blood running safely through your body."

"Don't patronize me," I said. I was glad I had never told him to call me by my first name. I crossed my arms over my chest and said, "I'll take your damn pills."

He stared at me hard. "Let's try this: here's a prescription for the Bisoprolol. Don't fill it. Cut each Enalapril in half; take a half-pill each day, instead of a whole pill. We'll review your blood results next week and go from there."

Was I hearing right? Had the high and mighty nurse practitioner listened to my opinion and conceded to my wishes?

I refused to give him the satisfaction of replying. Instead I asked, "How much did I weigh today?"

"You didn't read the digital display?"

"I was thinking instead of reading."

He bent his head down as if he were consulting his notes. When he looked up again, he asked, "Mr. Brown, if I irritate you, please tell me why."

I stood up. "Of course you irritate me. You force me to come here every week and remind me I am sick and dying, and there's nothing I can do about it."

He leaned back in his leather chair and folded his hands in his lap. "Yes. That is my job. But for what it's worth, we are all dying, whether we take note of it each week or not."

I rolled my eyes. "On that happy note, I'm leaving." I left the damn questionnaire on his desk.

I was out the door when I heard him call out, "201 pounds."

§§

Ryker did his impression of a telephone operator: "You have a call on line one, Mr. Brown."

I nodded to him and said to my customer, "If you'll excuse me, Mr. Reed, this won't take a moment." In fact, it would take less than a moment. Whoever was calling would get my "I'm sorry; I'm busy; I'll get back to you" reply, so I could return to my customer. I set out three different fragrances for the young stockbroker to try and picked up the department phone, with Ryker standing by nonchalantly to eavesdrop to my side of the conversation.

"Daddy, can you come meet me at Pottery Barn? I just bought a rug, and I need help getting it to the new apartment."

Damn. Chloé was the exception to my "I'm busy" rule. At least she knew to get to the point fast when I was at work, without any "Hello" or chitchat.

"Why can't George do it?"

"He's not answering."

I calculated, reviewed, looked for alternatives, and answered, "67 and Broadway?"

"Yes."

"15 minutes. 20 max."

She hung up before me, and Ryker nodded agreement that I was going to rush out.

Mr. Reed helped me by being decisive. He wanted the first of the colognes I had presented to him: Aventus by Creed, apple/jasmine/oakmoss, 1.7 ounces, $335. He charged it and left happy.

It was 5:03. With a miracle or two, I'd be back in 45 minutes and be able to wrap up another successful day. The first miracle came with an empty taxi waiting at the light on 58th Street and 6th Avenue just outside the employee exit.

At 67th Street, I told the driver to pull over and wait. I got out before he could complain and said, "You'll get a big tip."

I jay-walked across Broadway to Chloé standing on the sidewalk next to a rolled up rug that was taller than she was. I laughed because she looked like she was posing for a sculpture.

She greeted me with a grin and said, "It was on sale."

I squatted, put my arms around the bottom of the rug, and lifted. She held onto the other end, and together, we carried the rug like a giant sausage across Broadway, to where the driver was getting out of the cab.

"No, no, it's impossible," he cried. "That cannot go into my cab. No, stop."

It was too late. Chloé was smiling, saying, "It's no problem, really. It's just a few blocks. Look, it goes in like this." She was giggling wildly, on her knees on the back seat, pulling the front end of the rug into the taxi, pushing

225

the rug into the space in front of the back window. "See, it fits," she called out to the driver who stood in the street.

Truthfully, it didn't fit. Chloé backed out of the backseat, and we shoved my end of the rug as hard as we could. Finally, she rolled down the window and squeezed herself onto the edge of the seat. I closed the door with the rug sticking out of the window and ran around the back of the taxi to sit in the passenger seat.

Chloé called out of the corner of the open window to the driver on the sidewalk, "98ᵗʰ Street and West End Avenue, please." Her lilting voice transitioned into a tinkling laugh as she tried to arrange herself more comfortably underneath the rug.

The driver looked left and right, shot the bird at a car that honked as it swerved around his open door, and got in. Muttering under his breath, he put the cab in gear and burned rubber pulling into the lane of traffic.

At 98ᵗʰ Street, opening the door with the rug sticking out the window proved impossible. I opened the sidewalk-side door and maneuvered my end of the rug out of the back window space. Chloé pushed from the streetside window. I tugged until the damn thing finally slid onto the sidewalk.

Chloé jumped up and down with her arms in the air. "Success!!" she sang out. She ran around and hugged me, while I pulled out my wallet to pay the cabbie.

I tacked on a 30% tip. "Here's $20," I said to him, smiling sheepishly. "She's my daughter. What else can I say?" It had been the best part of my day.

After the cab adventure, carting the rug into the building and standing it up in the elevator was easy. It was 5:22. I silently thanked the apartment gods for getting Chloé out of a third-floor walk-up. I would have collapsed carrying the frigging rug up three flights of stairs.

At the 16th floor, we lifted it again from our respective ends and went to the apartment door on the left.

Chloé plunged her hand in her purse and pulled out keys.

"Do you like being a home-owner?"

"Daddy, it's fabulous. I love it. Imagine, only 3 apartments on the floor, and I'm one of them, with a view to die for."

"And your grandmother and Cary are the other two. It's not too much for you?"

She shook her head. "I think it's going to be great."

She held onto her end of the rug with one arm, put the key in the lock, and opened the door.

I took a step forward with the back end of the rug, but Chloé didn't budge. "Honey, let's …"

Before I could finish telling her to go inside so I could set the stupid rug down, I heard George's voice, "No, no, Chloé, no, it's not what you think."

My view inside the apartment was half-blocked by the rug, the door, and Chloé's back.

Chloé spoke in a tone that was so similar to Nana's ironic disdain that I felt a jolt of dread. She said, "I understand now why you couldn't answer the phone when I called."

Still in the doorway, she calmly set her end of the rolled-up rug on floor and took a step forward. That's when I heard a whimper from Babe, followed by the dog leaping over the rug, past Chloé, then past me, and dashing to the other end of the hallway to cower in front of Cary's closed door.

In the apartment, the scene was frozen. George stood in front of the couch in an unbuttoned blue work shirt, naked from there down, but the silhouette of what I had glimpsed when Chloé dropped the rug was singed into my brain.

"It wasn't my fault, Chloé, really. She'd been sniffing me all afternoon. For days, in fact. Her nose right there. She looked at me in that way, you know. It was clear; she wanted me. You know, in that way, she wanted me."

It sunk into my consciousness slowly that I was staring at the penis of my daughter's fiancé. It wasn't a pleasant sight.

"You're telling me that my grandmother's poodle asked to have sex with you?"

It was a bizarre group of words to hear together. It was the sort of line that would usually make Chloé laugh, the tinkling laugh of hers that could float over a room, lifting the spirit of everyone in range.

"It's not like I was screwing around on you. You know I wouldn't do that. I'm devoted to you. I love you, but we haven't had sex in weeks. I have no idea when you're going to 'feel normal' again." He held up two fingers of each hand when he said, "feel normal," as if they were quotations marks.

"You made Blue stand on the couch so you could …" she stopped, and I thought she was going to vomit. I thought I was going to vomit. The image of George standing behind Blue, grasping the thick curly hair of her haunches, flexing his hips again and again, how was I going to erase that image from my mind?

George shifted into gear. He ran around the living room gathering this shorts and jeans, putting them back on, buttoning his shirt, all the time jabbering, "She's just a dog, Chloé. Don't be such a prude. An animal. It's no different than masturbating. It's nothing. People have been doing it for centuries. You know, sheep or goats. Cows even. It's no big deal."

Chloé hadn't moved from her position in front of the rug. I wasn't sure she was breathing. I glanced to my right and saw Blue curled up in a ball at the far corner of the hallway next to Cary's door, trembling.

Chloé nodded. "An animal," she repeated. "George, you're the animal. And I don't live with animals. Put your shoes on and get out."

"Don't be stupid, Chloé," George said. "I haven't finished my workday. I don't have anywhere to go. I live here."

Her voice came out in a visceral growl that could have belonged to a hungry vampire. "Get out now. This instant. I'm going to call the police." The low vibration was more frightening than if she had screamed.

229

"That's stupid, Chloé. Don't act like this. Andy," George said, "you're a man. You understand. Explain to her."

I shook off my dazed stupor, dropped my end of the rug with a thud, and spoke: "You are a sick son of a bitch, and if you don't get out, she won't have to call the police because I'll hurt you so bad you won't ever fuck a woman again, much less a dog."

I took two steps forward and pushed Chloé out of the way. George side-stepped and grabbed his sneakers off the floor as he headed for the door. "Okay, okay. Take some time and cool down. I'll call you, Chloé. You'll see, this isn't a big deal. I'll be back tonight when you've had a chance to…"

We didn't hear how he ended the sentence because I slammed the door behind him. Chloé still stood without moving, her back toward me. Then I suddenly remembered, and jerked the door open in time to see George, at the end of the hallway, slamming his foot into Blue's side.

The dog screamed and bolted back down the hall into Chloé's apartment. Rage surged through me. Black, blinding rage, at seeing him attack the animal. I roared and ran toward George who had backed into the elevator. I watched him grinning as I impotently clawed at the closing door.

The dickhead was gone. I pulled out my cell phone and pushed the emergency call button.

When the dispatch person answered, I was almost calm enough to talk: "I'm reporting a physical and sexual assault. The man is leaving the building now."

The dispatcher was alert, quick, more than competent in taking the location and name of the assailant. He paused to dispatch the police to the scene, then asked me to describe George, what he was wearing, his age, and so forth. I gave my name and address, and was told someone would be on site soon.

It had not seemed relevant to tell the dispatcher that the victim was a Standard Poodle.

Inside the apartment, Chloé had sunk to the ground next to the new rug, crying, with her arms around a shivering Babe, and I sat down beside her.

All I could think to say was, "The police are coming."

Chloé wiped the back of her hand across her eyes. "I have to call someone to change the locks." She didn't move.

I nodded. There was no need for me to ask if the engagement was off. "If you want, I'll pack up his things and put them outside."

She shivered and said, "How did I ever let him touch me."

It was not a question.

The intercom buzzed, and Chloé looked at me, startled and scared.

I stood up and answered, "Yes?"

"It's the police. We had a call?"

"16th floor." I answered. "Please come up."

Chloé didn't move. I met the elevator and brought the two officers into the apartment, asking them to sit down.

They looked at me and started asking basic questions: names and what happened?

I outlined what I knew: "My daughter's…, " I couldn't bring myself to say the word "fiancé" so I substituted, "… daughter's boyfriend George Kuykendall was in the apartment alone. We came in with the new rug and found him…," again I had a hard time with words. What was I supposed to say? I leapt into the abyss, "…he was screwing the dog. My daughter told him to leave, and when he finally did, he kicked the dog…" that wasn't strong enough, I decided, and revised it, "…he kicked the dog savagely, in the hallway."

The younger cop looked at Chloé and asked, "Is that what happened?"

Chloé nodded, started crying again, and stammered, "He was naked, no, a shirt hanging, all wet, disgusting, the dog whimpered, screamed; he gripped her fur, pumping, oh my god," and she buried her face in Babe's neck.

The older police officer asked, "Do you know this man?"

I coughed out a mean laugh, "Obviously not well enough."

"Does he live here?"

Chloé answered, "He moved in a few days ago. We were dog-sitting. My grandmother's dog." She whinnied like a horse in pain, "Oh Daddy, what's Nana going to say? How could I have let this happen?" She covered her face with her hands.

The younger officer leaned forward and said, "Ms. Brown, this is not your fault."

I affirmed what the woman said, "She's right, Chloé. This is not your fault."

The older cop said, "Probably the dog's okay, but as a precaution, a trip to the vet is a good idea. Ask him take photos and send us a record of the exam."

Chloé blinked several times, wiped her eyes, and asked, "Can you do anything? I mean, this is bound to be illegal, right? Animal abuse or something?"

The young cop replied, "Oh, we already have the man in custody."

My mouth dropped open. "You caught him?"

"Whoever called must have done it fast. He was apprehended on the subway platform at 96th Street. He's on his way to the precinct now."

The older officer explained, "New York has strict laws against injuring or torturing an animal. It's a Class A misdemeanor. Also, sexual misconduct includes having sex with an animal, another Class 'A' offense. Each conviction carries up to a year in jail plus a $1,000 fine. Will you press charges?"

Chloé's hands went up to her chest, and she gasped like she was having a heart attack.

"Chloé?" I asked. "What's wrong? Are you sick?"

She nodded, "No. I mean, no, I'm okay. Yes, charges. I hope he is convicted; he needs to be in jail."

The officers stood up, and the older one handed me a card. "Call us if you have questions."

The younger one told Chloé, "We'll be in contact."

We were silent after the door closed behind the police officers.

Finally, I said, "We should get Babe to the veterinarian."

She raised her eyes to me and moaned, "I need to call Nana and tell her."

"That'll be a surprise anniversary gift," I said sarcastically. "Wait until we get back from the vet."

"You think Babe can stand up?" she asked, coaxing the poodle to move.

I looked at my watch. "It's already 6:25. I'll call the vet's office to let them know we're on the way with an emergency."

We managed to get out of the building with Babe limping, and found a cab that let the three of us in the back seat.

§§

It was near 8:00 o'clock by the time we returned from the vet's office with a report about her examination. The results for her vaginal/rectal exam would be ready in four days, and we had a week's worth of Previcox pain medication for her bruised ribs.

On the 16th floor, I took charge, "We're not going back in your apartment, not until the locks are changed. And you're not staying alone."

"But George is probably in jail, Daddy; I'll be okay."

Chloé words contradicted the shakiness in her voice. She looked like she'd been whipped.

I used my parent tone of voice to say: "I want Babe to be where she's most comfortable. We'll stay in Nana's apartment." I juggled through my keys and found the right one. Inside, Chloé locked the door, and Blue retreated into Nana's bedroom.

"I'm starving," I said. "We'll order in, and I'll find a locksmith who can come tomorrow morning. When do you have to be at work?"

I looked at my phone, and there it was: a text from Ryker asking where I was. Oh, right, I hadn't called to say I wasn't returning to work. Well, he had figured it out, I was sure, though I'd bet my life's salary that he couldn't guess why I hadn't shown up.

§§

I ate my sweet and sour pork from a plate on the lamp table. Chloé was curled on the sofa eating Kung Pao Chicken with chopsticks from the box, holding her mobile next to her ear with her shoulder.

"Of course, the 'wedding' is off, Nana," she said. "There was never going to be a wedding. You should have known that."

She listened, and I tried to imagine how Nana was responding to the tale Chloé had told her.

Chloé replied, "It was a party. A million people were here, he asked them to watch, and nobody noticed that I didn't answer when he popped the question."

Chloé closed her eyes as if she were silently groaning inside while she listened from her end of the conversation.

"What was I supposed to do with a crowd of witnesses cheering him on?" she said. "They threw themselves into a celebration as if it were a game show."

She stayed silent for a couple of minutes, and nodded in between taking mouthfuls of chicken.

"The vet said she'd be okay, Nana. But I don't know. It was such a trauma."

She listened, and I waited.

"No, don't cut your trip short. Daddy's here. He's not going to let me be alone. I'll sleep in your bed tonight next to Babe, if that's okay with you."

She paused, looked at me, then said into the phone, "Do you want to talk to him?"

Nana must have said No.

"Okay, I'll tell him. I'll call you tomorrow. My love to Cary."

"So you never meant to marry George?" I asked after my eavesdropping.

She took a gulp of iced tea. "If he'd asked me in private like a normal person, I would have said No. As it worked out, I figured I'd find the right time to give the stupid ring back to him."

I didn't understand. "But you moved in with him."

She nodded and swallowed. "We got along, but I don't *LOVE* him." She underlined the word "love" with a yodel in her voice. "He was boyfriend material, not husband material." She sighed and added, "I'm not sure anyone is husband material." She said the last thing with her eyes focused inside the Chinese food box.

"Is that because of your mother and me?" I asked.

She shrugged and chewed.

"You might be right, Chloé." It was my turn to sigh. "I know it seemed like your mother abandoned us, and I know it was hard on you, but my life has been easier without a spouse watching and judging me all the time. I'm glad she left."

I took a bite of pork. When the silence went on too long, I said, "And it wasn't your mother's fault."

"Daddy, come on. I know Mother as well as you do. She's flighty and selfish and superficial."

I couldn't argue any of that, but I could tell the truth. "Yes, but she had a reason to leave. I cheated on her. It was a client from Bergdorf's, and your mother found out, and she couldn't stay after that."

Chloé's mouth hung open. I saw it on her face, the re-calculating, the recalibrating of all she had believed about her mother, and about me.

"No one ever told me," she whispered.

I decided not to use the excuse that I had been protecting her with my silence. Nana didn't know either. The reality was that my silence had protected me and my shiny image of the selfless, loving father.

"I was stupid. Men make mistakes. Mine was huge, and it cost you your mother."

I stared at her, hoping she'd say she forgave me, but my daughter couldn't look at me.

"She didn't want me with her?" Chloé mumbled the half-question with her face buried between her hunched shoulders.

"Oh honey, she wanted you. She loved you. She is who she is, but she loved you completely. She still loves you with all her heart. Her leaving wasn't your fault. We thought with Nana here, it was better for you to stay with me so you could finish high school with your friends.

That's all. You've always been the center of her life, no matter where she is."

She sighed, like the world was dissolving around her. "I guess I need to call her in California and tell her there won't be a baby or a wedding." She sniffled and wiped her nose with the back of her hand. "That's a lot of news at once."

I gritted my teeth. Tanya knew about the abortion because I had told the story without Chloé's permission -- one more reason for my daughter to be mad at me. Maybe I could keep my finger in the dyke: "I'll call her for you, if you want."

She nodded agreement, and I knew I had escaped another noose of my own making.

I wouldn't have thought it was possible, but Chloé's face dropped one level lower into misery, and she said sadly, "Daddy, George was the reason I didn't want the baby. I didn't admit it out loud, but I knew, he wasn't a good choice long-term. He wasn't a man I respected; he wasn't a father-man."

I was sure my daughter didn't respect me either. I wasn't a father-man. I was a shit. That was the side-effect of telling the truth about the affair that had ruined my marriage. Okay, yes, it was a marriage that had giant cracks, but I was the one that broke it open. I was the one who had shattered the chance for my daughter to finish her adolescence with a normal family life. Because of my bad choices, she doubted anyone could be "husband material."

I shook off my self-pity and turned my thoughts back to George, the guy she did not want to marry. I started to say, "So, he was just a good lay?" and immediately decided that was not a daughter/father conversation to have. Instead, I said, "You're a smart woman," and left it at that.

She rolled her eyes like that was a bunch of horseshit, but she let my statement stand.

The conversation reverberated in the silence, until finally, we moved forward. I cleared up the left-over Chinese food, while Chloé went to Nana's room.

I found a blanket, took off my Ferragamo loafers and Magnanni belt, and stretched out on the couch. Then I dialed Tanya in California. It was a short call, without many details, other than, "George and Chloé broke up." But I added, "Come to New York soon, even though there's no event on the calendar. I think Chloé would like to see you."

§§

It took four days for the locksmith to show up. Slow and expensive: that was how it was in New York City. The same day, Nana and Cary got back from Block Island. With them as bodyguards and new locks on Chloé's door, I returned to my apartment.

Nana called me to say that Chloé had made a date to go see a movie with Ned.

"Ned?" I asked. "Do I know him?"

"Yes, you know him," she chided me. "He gave you tickets to the ballet, remember?"

I was shocked. I had figured that Chloé would be in mourning for a while, what with the perverted assault on Babe and her broken engagement.

"Apparently, Cary mentioned to Ned at the gym that Chloé wasn't seeing George anymore, and he asked for her phone number."

I wondered how much Cary had shared at the gym. Was the bizarre story of my daughter's fiancé's arrest buzzing around the exercise machines?

"I hope she has a nice time," I said in a neutral voice. "How is Babe doing?"

Nana was silent for a minute. "To be honest, she's a nervous wreck. She's clingy and hesitant and doesn't want to eat or go out."

I didn't want to give a French Poodle the same status as a human being, but her reaction made sense to me after what she'd gone through. "With time, she'll return to normal," I said, not quite believing myself. "Anyhow, I'm sure she's glad you're back. Chloé too." I started to say good-bye, and paused. "Me too," I added, and signed off.

§§

I showed up early at Ponytail's office, and I sat down in the hallway to wait.

Chloé was on my mind: the pregnancy and termination, the marriage proposal, her fiancé out on bail for sexual assault and locked out of my daughter's new home forever, and her knowing about my infidelity that had silently shaped her adolescence and adulthood.

The words that haunted me most were, "She didn't want me with her?" Chloé had thought her mother didn't want her, didn't love her. To a child, that was the obvious conclusion because there wasn't enough information to know the whole adult picture.

How much had that misunderstanding formed Chloé's view of the world, of its potential for security or for love? I hated thinking about it, and couldn't stop thinking about it.

The door opened and an old woman left Ponytail's office. Old? I laughed. She might have been a couple of years older than I.

Ponytail signaled me inside and jumped into our session. I was ruminating about Chloé's childhood conclusions and traumas while he took my blood pressure. I'd had my own anguish when I was young, but of course, I had long ago gotten past it. I had told myself to move on.

"130/89," he announced as he took the BP wrap off my arm.

"Maybe high blood pressure runs in my family," I said.

"That's not high, Mr. Brown. It's good for a man your age with heart disease."

"No, I mean, I never gave you a family history. We talk about my weight and my arteries, and maybe all this is hereditary."

He directed me to stand on the scales. "Your mother gave us your family history when you were in the hospital. It's all in your dossier."

"My mother?" I gawked. "But she's not.…"

"Yes, I know. She told us you were adopted as an infant. So we don't know your entire history."

I stood up straight. I felt my eyes bulge out. "She told you that?"

Ponytail stepped back and looked at me with surprise. "You knew, didn't you?"

I stammered, then stuttered, and finally said, "Yes. Yes, of course, but…, why would she.…" It was perfectly natural that she would tell a doctor what she knew about my medical background in an emergency situation: blood type, previous operations, prior heart problems, diabetes in the family or not, and so on.

I took a breath, "Usually she doesn't mention it. She didn't even tell me until my father died."

Ponytail looked at me sideways and returned to his chair behind his desk. "What did he die of?" he asked.

I looked at the weight flashing on the digital screen in front of me, 196, and I stepped off the scales. "He had a heart attack on the golf course. He was dead by the time they got him to the hospital."

"How old was he?"

I shrugged. I wasn't sure. "I was 15 when it happened. But he wasn't my real father, so it doesn't have any connection to my heart attack." Of course, back when he died, I thought he was my father. I had swallowed Nana's lie about my birth for 15 years. Well, not a lie. An omission.

"I was just curious," Ponytail said. "Your mother must have some emotional scars from losing her husband like that, then seeing the same thing happen to her son."

"My mother hated his passion for golf."

"You never searched for your natural parents?" he asked, while typing notes on his tablet.

At 15, I had been moving to the end of adolescence, not far off from being an adult, when Nana told me that she wasn't my real mother. I had been shocked. Sort of miffed. And confused. But she was my mother, ever since my first bottle of formula, just like Dad had been my father. There wasn't anything to go search for. What would I have said if I had found my birth mother? Why didn't you want me? Why did you give me away? Oh my god, I sounded like Chloé.

"No," I answered Ponytail. For decades, I had imagined and accepted the most logical explanation: that my birth mother had been in high school, without a choice beyond abortion or giving the baby away. Why would I need to know more than that?

"And your adoptive parents, do you know why they chose to adopt?"

"My dad was sterile." Nana had told me that much. She didn't say why. It could have been because of agent orange, or a vasectomy, or a tumor, or whatever. Apparently she thought she had told her 15 year old enough, and that was that.

Ponytail closed his notebook and folded his hands on his desk. "You don't tell many people about your adoption, do you?"

It didn't sound like an accusation, more like he wanted confirmation for his assumption.

"No," I answered. "No one." That was true. I couldn't think of anyone who knew. It was not a story that Nana repeated, and me, I had not referred to my being adopted when I was in love, or drunk, or angry, or anytime at all, not even to my wife or my daughter. It wasn't a secret. I didn't see that it mattered enough to mention.

§§

It was almost a habit, me stopping by the top floor at Bergdorf's to visit Dominic Berlini. At the beginning of the week, I dropped off slacks or a jacket for alteration, and picked up the like-new clothing on Friday.

"What do you have for me this time?" Dominic greeted me, without saying Hello.

"My grey worsted suit," I said, handing him a bag. "My daughter's birthday is coming up and I want to take her out this weekend."

Dominic ran his fingers over the fabric, caressing it, judging it. Then he looked me up and down, from his low viewpoint. "You've lost weight again. I'll have to take measurements."

He pointed me to stand on the fitting platform and motioned for me to take off my jacket. He stood on his stool, lifted the tape measure from around his neck, and began measuring me, jotting numbers in his pocket notebook. It was strangely like being in Ponytail's office, with my body being observed, touched, gauged, and judged.

"Where are you taking her?" he asked. "For her birthday?"

I smiled. "I thought we'd get dinner at Carolines on Broadway for dinner and the show."

Dominic stopped measuring and took pins out of his mouth. "Are you crazy?" he asked.

"What?" I shot back, indignant. "My birthday's two weeks after Chloé's so it's a night for both of us."

He turned his head up at a 90° angle so he could look me in the eyes. "That's okay. But why would you wear funeral clothes to a birthday celebration? This suit! Oh no, you can't wear this suit. I'll alter it, but you have to buy something new for a night out like that. Something young. Something you can move in." He held his palms up like he had finished the conversation with his definitive statement, put the pins back in his mouth, and continued to measure my body parts.

I thought for a second. "So you think I need to look more casual?"

He kept at his work and mumbled something that sounded affirmative. Maybe he was right. After all, I was only 52 years old, going on 53, not 83. I could look good and have fun next to my 27 year old daughter. Why not?

When I stepped down from the fitting platform, I slapped Dominique on the shoulder. "Thanks. You're right. I'm going over now to find birthday clothes."

"Of course, I'm right. See you Friday," and he carried off my suit.

§§

I had 30 minutes before the store opened. In the Men's Store, I looked around, homed in on a young salesman stocking shirts on a shelf, and told him about my birthday project.

He introduced himself, "I'm Joey Belton." I didn't know him. "How old's your daughter?" he asked. When I told him, he grinned and said, "Do you need a chaperone?" I didn't laugh, and he back-pedaled, "Just joking."

"Do you know Carolines on Broadway?"

"Sure," he said, giving me a once over.

"What should I wear?" I hoped he wouldn't suggest thongs and baggy pants hanging on my hips that showed my underwear.

Luckily, he came up with something I liked after only three tries: McQueen straight legged black jeans and an Armani long-sleeved, olive-color T-shirt.

He led me back to the counter, but stopped short in his tracks and turned his head. "You know, I have a sport coat marked down ½ price. It'd be perfect with the jeans and t-shirt, if you'd like to see it."

How could the kid be so young and use a vintage sales technique like that? I'd used it with customers for years.

"You're a 38 regular, right?" he asked and didn't wait for an answer.

I hadn't been a 38 regular in my entire life.

Joey took a tan cotton twill jacket off a hanger and held it for me to slip into.

"That's some lining," I said about the jungle and parrot pattern of the lining.

He smiled and posed me in front of a mirror. "Perfect fit," he said with a shrug.

Damn, he was right. I tried to hide my surprise. "I'll take it," I said, "And Joey, add on another t-shirt like the olive one, but another color."

"I have it in dark grey, navy, and aqua-marine."

Dark grey would go well with the black jeans. "Let's go with the aqua-marine," I said, pleased with the choice.

He arranged for the sealed bag to be waiting for me at the employee exit, and I rushed to work in the Women's Store.

§§

I made three sales by rote, listened to Faith's tale about her mother's swelling ankles, and took a break. The shopping bug had bitten me. I cruised through the store, and like a magnet was pulling me, I landed in front of the first floor jewelry counter that held my white-gold Son of Poseidon signet ring.

"It's a handsome piece," Frank Bryson said.

I recognized a sales pitch when I heard one. It didn't have to have a lot of razzle dazzle, just something to make the customer agree and begin salivating. As a salesperson myself, I was easy prey.

I nodded and replied, "You're right." If I tried the ring on again, I wouldn't leave without it. It was made for me. I imagined my new olive t-shirt and tan sport coat finished by the ring on my hand. It would be the perfect birthday present to myself. I managed to say, "I'll be back," and commanded my feet to take me upstairs for a cup of coffee.

The cup was half-empty when the ring flashed in my mind again. By the time I took the last sip of coffee, I knew what I was going to do.

I road the elevator to the first floor and found Frank in his usual pose behind the counter.

"I need your help," I told him. "But I need to keep it between us." I knew I was asking the impossible. Bergdorf

251

Goodman was a Petrie dish of hot gossip, all masquerading as "passing along a good story about someone you don't know."

I repeated the operative word, "Confidential. Can you do confidential? For me? For this one thing?"

Frank was an expert at growing things in the BG Petrie dish. He shifted his eyes to the side as if he were actually considering my question. Then he said, "It depends. What kind of thing are we talking about? Money? Sex?" He raised his eyebrows and suggested, "Murder? I'd love a good story about murder."

I shook my head. "Not murder. About health. My health. Something about my health that would be… ah… would be embarrassing if it got around. I might sound like an invalid," I rushed on, "which I am not! Absolutely not!"

Frank chewed on his forefinger's cuticle. "It's obvious you're no invalid. In fact, you look better than I could have imagined possible." He gave me the once over. "Your color is good. Your clothes finally have some glitz and style. Your hair has always been thick, even though it's receding….which is no fair." He smoothed the hair over his ears which was all he had.

"So?" I asked. "You'll keep this to yourself?"

He hedged, "I promise I'll do my best. That's all I can say since I don't know yet what it is."

That would have to be good enough. I spilled my beans: "My doctor wants me to get a gizmo that I can punch for help if I have another heart attack. I checked it

252

out on the internet. It's tiny. Can you design a ring for me that could house the damn thing?"

"Let me see it," Frank demanded.

I pulled out my phone, did a search for the gizmo, and handed him the cell.

He scrolled, read, and replied: "Not a ring. It's too ugly. You could hang it from a necklace and keep it inside your shirt. But I bet you'd take it off as soon as you got home and would forget to put it back on. A bracelet maybe, but do you want to wear a bracelet 24/7?"

I felt my shoulders slump. I agreed with him. The gizmo was ugly, and just big enough to be noticeable.

"My suggestion," Frank went on, "would be to make it into an ankle bracelet. It's waterproof, so you can bathe with it. You could hide it under your sock most of the time. I imagine you'd get used to it, like a convict with an electronic tracking bracelet on his ankle."

It'd be out of sight most of the time so it wouldn't have to be a gorgeous piece of expensive jewelry. I could reach it on my ankle if I fell. "I like the idea. Yes."

"You get me the gizmo, and I'll have one of our designers make the ankle bracelet. Stainless steel?" he askcd.

"Whatever you think, Frank. I trust your judgement." I smirked and added "Only, no diamonds, okay?"

"You're no fun," he smirked in return.

"I mean it, thanks," I said sincerely.

Frank leaned toward me over the counter and said in a conspiratorial voice, "The bracelet will be cheap, but you'll owe me."

I knew what he meant. Like most of the personnel, he knew the value of perfume testers. "I'll have something for you by the end of the day."

"That's my man," he said.

§§

At home, I dumped my change from the blue crystal vase on the middle of the bed. A few weeks back, the money in my gym bag had been $52 short of $3,000. I separated, rolled, and tallied the new quarters, dimes, nickels, and pennies: $593.83. I rounded down for a grand total of $3540.

The next morning, I shouldered the gym bag and passed by PNB Bank. "Good morning," I said to the teller. "I'd like to deposit these coins in my checking account please."

The young blond bit her lip, and I assumed she was restraining herself from making jokes about my life savings.

§§

Chloé came directly from work to meet me at Carolines at Broadway and 50th Street. She had circles under her eyes. Maybe I did too. We'd both seen a lot of drama recently.

When we were at the table, I opened the menu and asked her, "Did you make good progress with your clients today?" Why did people do that? Why did I do it, asking a question just when we needed silence to read and decide on what food to order?

Luckily, Chloé ignored me and concentrated on the menu. When the waiter came back, she said, "The impossible burger comes with fries, right?" The waiter nodded. She pushed her red glasses up on her nose and continued, "So, the impossible burger, mustard, no mayo, and a Budweiser. Can you bring a carafe of water too, please?"

The waiter jotted notes on his pad and turned to me. I'd had a hard time deciding between the baby back ribs and the chicken parmesan. I went with the parm. "And a glass of Zinfandel," I added.

Chloé sat up straight and answered my original question with a smile, "One patient finished his work with me today. Seven months since a car accident that broke both his legs and also required a hip replacement. Now he wants to join his company's softball team."

"Thanks to you," I said proudly.

Her lilting laugh swept over me, "Thanks to me."

The waiter brought our drinks. After he left, Chloé leaned toward me with her eyes twinkling above the dark circles. "But that's not the best news of the day."

"Of course not," I said. "It's your birthday. That's the best."

She wagged her head with a smile, "No, not that. Yes, that's good, but this is better. The patent lawyer called me today. The U.S. Patent Office granted my patent! You are sitting with an official patent holder. That is, after I pay the issuance fee for the patent number." She waved her hand in the air and went on, "But that's no big deal. The patent will be published and legal in about a month."

I took a sip of wine. "How much is the issuance fee?"

"The lawyer said between $500 and $700. That's cheap compared to the original filing fee."

I replaced my white cloth napkin on the table. "I'm going to the men's room. I'll be right b ack."

I went to the back of the dining room and signaled to our waiter. At the door of the kitchen, I told him, "Hi," and read his nametag. "Jerry, it's my daughter's birthday. After we finish eating, will you bring out the Brownie Sundae for her and the Apple Tart for me?"

From the inside pocket of my tan jacket I pulled out two envelopes. Handing him the unsealed one, I explained, "Here are some birthday candles. If you can put them on the sundae and light them, I'd appreciate it."

"No problem," the waiter said.

Then I handed him the other envelope, the sealed one. "This is her gift, Jerry. Could you put it on the plate? Or under the plate? Or something like that?"

He grinned and said, "I'll figure something out."

I turned to walk away, and the waiter coughed meaningfully.

When I looked around, he said "Uh, I'm a singer." He ducked his head in embarrassment, "Unemployed at the moment. I'd be happy to sing to your daughter…, if you want, that is."

It was my turn to grin. "Her name is Chloé, and you can look forward to a big tip. You should know, my birthday is in two weeks."

That made him laugh.

I sat down across from Chloé, and immediately the unemployed singer/waiter brought out our food. The pomodoro sauce over my chicken parmesan smelled like a magic potion of onion and basil.

We toasted each other, saying, "Salut," as if we were in Italy, and sipped wine and beer. Then Chloé sank her teeth into the giant veggie burger, and I took a bite of the parm.

I sighed at the same time as Chloé. She laughed liltingly and said, "We must be related." She swallowed and added, "There's something orgasmic about eating good food."

I swallowed in my turn. "It's one of the great pleasures in the world." I cut another bite, but before I ate

258

it, I said, "Your dog leash design is great, Chloé. I know the main attraction is the elastic give that makes it easy on the joints, but I love the way each seven-inch section lets me hold Blue as close or as loose as I want. Is the same company going to keep manufacturing it now that you have the patent?"

"I don't know. The lawyer warned me that individuals and companies both would contact me soon, trying to make deals with me."

"You may be able to retire soon," I joked.

Chloé laughed lightly and kept eating.

"Any other inventions on the horizon?" I asked.

"Nothing like the leash," she said. "But I started research for an article on post-heart attack weight loss and gain. You were the one who gave me the idea. I hope you don't mind."

What could I say? "Will my name be in it?" I half wanted her to say Yes; a little notoriety could be a good thing.

Her laugh tinkled across the table. "Maybe I'll dedicate it to you. It'll take a while. I'm canvassing 5,000 recovering heart-attack patients with a questionnaire about habits they changed after their hospitalizations."

"I'll fill one out if you want."

She shook her head. "Sorry, no relatives allowed. It might skew the results."

I admired Chloé. She was smart, not just school-smart, but imaginative-smart and people-smart, and she was light-hearted about it. Usually her scientific work was over my head, and I didn't bother to read more than the title, but this sounded interesting. "I'd like to read it when you have a draft finished," I said.

"Absolutely," she replied. "In my opinion, not just as your daughter, but as someone associated with the medical field, you are awesome, Daddy. In six months, you have transformed yourself. You look healthy, and slim, and by the way, that's a great jacket you have on."

I preened like a cock in the hen-house that she had noticed the size 38R sport coat.

"Speaking of slim, I've been meaning to ask you…," I was going to say Ponytail wanted me to get some exercises, but I couldn't remember his real name, "… ah, you remember the, ah, nurse practitioner…"

She swished another French fry in ketchup and said, "Sure, Bradley Matthews, at Mount Sinai West."

There it was: his name. Bradley Matthews.

I went on, "Yes. He told me you might have some exercises for me that would tighten up my skin after the weight loss." I felt my face flush from embarrassment. I probably looked red enough to be having another heart attack, just from asking for help.

Luckily, Chloé kept a poker face. "I never thought I'd say it twice in one day, but 'no relatives allowed'." She tilted her head to the side and gave me a soft smile. "But I have a colleague you'll really like, Terry Mayor. He owes me a favor; I'll get him to meet with you a couple of times at no charge. He'll know what you need to do."

I was still chagrined, but I managed to say, "If you think it's a good idea."

"It's a wonderful idea. I'll give him your phone number, okay?"

I nodded and swiped a piece of Italian bread through the sauce on my plate while I searched for a subject to switch to. Ah! "Tell me about the date you had with Ned, Cary's friend from the gym."

She was ¾ finished with her burger and had six or seven fries left. I loved the way she rationed her meal, so she polished off all the different foods at the same time. It had been her habit since she was five years old.

"I think I told you, he took me to see *Downton Abbey, a New Era*. I thought it was a funny choice, but the movie wasn't bad. We went out again a couple of nights ago. He took me to walk the High Line, and we ate at Brunetti Pizza afterwards."

I'd eaten a fair amount of my chicken parm, but the plate was still covered in spaghetti. I signaled the waiter and asked for the rest to be put in a doggy bag. Chloé's plate was empty.

The waiter gave me a conspiratorial smile and said, "Do you want to see the dessert menu?"

I glanced at his nameplate again, but before I could say anything to Jerry, Chloé answered, "Yes, please." She looked at her watch and asked me, "We have time before the show, don't we?"

I nodded, and Jerry left.

"It sounds like Cary's young friend likes you," I said.

"Ned?" Chloé shrugged. "He's nice, but I won't go out with him again. He's sort of insecure and tedious. But he was… well, he was a shot of anesthesia I needed after George. You understand?"

I wouldn't have minded if she had linked up with Ned and the New York City Ballet crowd, but I certainly understood the need for temporary escape. I was still wounded from the abortion, marriage proposal, perverted attack on Babe, and break up, and none of it had happened to me. What Chloé was going through must be ten times more difficult. A hundred times more difficult.

"Keep taking good care of yourself, honey. If there's anything I can do, let me know. Anything at all."

She reached across the table and patted my hand. I wasn't sure in the dimness of the Supper Lounge, but I thought her eyes were watering.

"*Happy birthday to you*," a light baritone voice glided through the air toward us, "*happy birthday to you, happy birthday dear Chloé, happy birthday to you…,*" the song wasn't finished, "*…and to Daddy too*."

By the end, Chloé was laughing, the unemployed singer/waiter stood beside our table, and my grin was as big as I could get it. Jerry put two desserts on the table. He'd stuck eight candles on Chloé's Brownie Sundae, jutting out in all directions, and five candles were jabbed into my Apple Tart. He took out a lighter, and in less than a minute, we had a festival of candlelight on the table.

"On the count of three, make a wish, and blow out your candles," Jerry said to both of us. Then dramatically, he counted: "One…, two…, three!"

Chloé and I paused, wished, and blew. I thought I was going to have to take a second breath, but the stubborn fifth candle finally went out. I didn't ask what Chloé wished, but I hoped it would come true for her. She deserved whatever she wanted.

As for me, I wished for fun. It was silly, yes, but yes, I wanted more fun in my life. I loved work and had fun there, and I had good-natured friends and family, but I needed more. Maybe the candle gods had something in mind for me.

Jerry applauded our success and asked, "Coffee?

"Yes, please," Chloé said.

"Decaf for me," I answered.

We had each taken the first bite of dessert when Jerry returned. He set my decaf next to my tart. Then he gallantly placed a folded, bright yellow napkin on Chloé's side of the table, and put her coffee on top of it.

"What's that?" Chloé asked, pointing to the napkin.

Jerry smiled enigmatically. "You're our 10,000th birthday guest, so you get a yellow napkin."

Chloé pursed her lips suspiciously and pulled the paper napkin out from under the saucer. She felt it, measuring its thickness. She sniffed it. Finally she unfolded it and found the white envelope. Jerry backed away while she looked him as if he were a bad little boy.

Chloé slit open the envelope with her finger and pulled out a check. Her eyes popped wide open, "My god, Daddy. That's a lot of money!"

I had tried to come up with some magic number, maybe the sum of the numbers of her birthday, or her age times my age, but I couldn't find the right combination. So I had kept it simple and written her a check for $3,200.

"I had some extra money sitting around," I said casually, without explaining about my blue vase full of coins for the Son of Poseidon ring. "I used part of it for this." I stuck my leg out from under the table, pulled the hem of my new black jeans up, and pulled down my sock.

"You're going steady with someone who gave you an ankle bracelet?" she quipped.

"No. It's a panic button. *Nurse Matthews* suggested it," I said disdainfully, "just in case I ever have another heart problem. After getting this gizmo, I had money left over, so I thought you could find something to spend it on. Happy birthday, Chloé."

The look on my daughter's face was worth every cent. I'd continue tossing my change in the blue vase and buy a ring for myself later.

She held the check to her chest, half-stood out of her chair, and kissed my cheek. "Thank you, Daddy. I'll find something special to do with it."

"Let me know when you decide." I'd done well with her gift, and I felt like I was president of the world. I pulled up my sock and pointed, "I'll tell you a secret about these socks."

She was savoring another bite of the Brownie Sundae, so she silently nodded, indicating she wanted to know.

"They're not from Bergdorf Goodman." I grinned when she almost choked on the chocolate.

"But Daddy, everything you wear is from Bergdorf's. It's like you are Mr. Bergdorf himself. And Mr. Goodman too, both rolled into one. What do you mean, not from Bergdorf Goodman?"

I leaned in close. "Not my boxer shorts either."

She burst out laughing so loudly that the people at the table next to us looked over.

I whispered my secret, "I buy them at Target."

Still laughing, she grabbed her heart and said, "Oh my god, I'm going to have a heart attack. When have you ever gone in a Target?"

I sipped my decaf and replied, "I order them on-line from the Target at Herald Square. That way when I pick them up, no one recognizes me like they would at the Target near me on 61st Street and Broadway. The M7 bus goes down there."

She wagged her head like I was ruining her vision of reality.

I explained, "At Bergdorf, Versace boxers are $150 a pair. The cheapest brand is $15 a pair. At Target, I get five Fruit of the Loom boxers, any color I want, for $20." I repeated myself for emphasis, "Five for $20."

"And socks?" Chloé pressed.

I grinned as if I were hiding stolen diamonds. "Instead of $290 for a pair of Brioni cotton crew socks…," I paused while Chloé gagged with her hands at her throat, "… or even $18 for BG basic black socks, at Target I get 10 pairs for $12. Yes!" and I pumped my fist.

"So that's how you saved $3,200 to give to me?"

"Well, no," I shrugged. "But I get a kick out of retrieving my secret socks from the pick-up desk at the 34th Street Target. You won't tell anyone, will you?" I whispered.

"And ruin your BG reputation? Never," she replied.

I looked at my watch. "We've got 20 minutes before showtime. No rush; our seats are reserved."

We finished the desserts and coffee; then I signaled Jerry for the bill. He handed me a doggy bag full of spaghetti and chicken parmesan, and I tapped my card on the charge machine, including a very large tip.

§§

A young woman led us into the theater, through a narrow aisle, to a table just to the right of the stage-platform. The room was shadowy with spotlights and candles, full of people chatting and laughing and waiting for the comedian.

"What can I get you to drink?" the young woman asked.

Young woman? Ha. She looked the same age as Chloé.

My daughter glanced at me with a twinkle in her eye and asked lightly, "Am I still celebrating my birthday?"

I nodded. "Have anything you want."

She turned to the young woman, "I'll have Kahlua over ice, please."

I put in my order: "I'll have seltzer with lemon."

Chloé didn't remark about my choice like Ryker or Faith would have. It was a good idea for me to skip the Sambuca and sherry. I'd eaten heavy food, it was getting close to my normal bedtime, and I didn't want to fall asleep during the second half of the big birthday night.

The lights dimmed and a spotlight flashed on the microphone in the middle of the stage. A skinny man with a goatee made his way to the platform. "Good evening, ladies and gentlemen and everyone else too." That line earned him a groan from the crowd. "Don't worry. Tonight,

Carolines has someone a lot funnier than me. If you've seen her before, on T.V., in the movies, or even on stage, you know how fabulous she is. Without making you wait any longer, here's Issa Rae's best friend, Chris Rock's opening act, the author of *Bamboozled by God*, let's have a loud welcome for Yvonne Orji!"

The skinny man jumped off-stage, and a black woman with long braided hair danced up the three small stairs to the stage. She wore a tight black t-shirt down to her thighs. The audience went wild, clapping and whistling.

Behind the microphone, she said, "Hi there, everybody. Hello." She gave little waves toward this person and that as if she knew some people in the crowd. She interrupted the noise to say, "I'm Yvonne Orji. Do you like my maroon tights?" She mimed a model styling hosiery, running her long fingernails up and down her leg. The crowd howled and clapped wildly. "I like them too," she said. "It's obvious; we're going to have a fantastic night together." The audience roared again. Orji was already in charge, and Chloé's face was radiant as she laughed out loud.

"It's not just my legs that are great," Orji said without smiling. "My arms work well too. You know, like when I'm walking along the New York City sidewalk at lunchtime? It's packed with people all leaving their 78-story office buildings to find a food cart for a 15 minute meal, and me, I'm going the other direction." She mimed trying to walk forward with a crowd pushing her in the other direction, as if she were in hurricane force winds.

"They expect me to shrink over to the side so they can keep surging forward. After all, I'm small and insignificant. But they don't know my Superpower."

Her eyes flashed. "I have elbows." She raised her fists chest high with her elbows out to the side. "All I have to do is walk like this, and you should see the crowd open up to let me pass through. It's like Moses and the Red Sea, or a linebacker for the Giants -- it's a linebacker who passes other players doing this, right? -- or my mother trying to dance disco."

The audience laughed at each phrase. Her expressions and timing were natural and hilarious. "If someone gets too close to me, bam! A sharp elbow bone jabs 'em. I love that." The crowd roared. "I learned the technique when I was in junior high playing basketball." She whacked her elbows to the left and the right. Then she leaned forward and whispered into the microphone, "And you should know, it works with men who get overly frisky, and on crowded subways too."

I wiped my eyes from laughing so hard, took a sip of my sparkling water, and felt someone touch my arm. I shifted and saw Shannon Shriver squatting down next to me.

"I noticed you from back there," she said softly, nodding her head to the left. "Let's talk after the show."

I nodded, and she disappeared. I turned my attention back to the stage and caught Chloé grinning at me with her eyebrows lifted almost to her hairline. I rolled my eyes and ignored her. But my concentration was broken.

Orji's comic routine went on with a story about throwing up on Lil Rel Howery's shoes, and another about asking her 15 year old boyfriend to marry her, being turned down, and getting revenge a decade later. I heard it all, but I was distracted. I tried not to scan the crowd to see where Shannon was sitting, and unfortunately, I was successful.

When the set was finished, the well-deserved applause went on and on. Chloé hooted and clapped, and then she leaned against my shoulder to say, "Best birthday yet, Daddy. Thanks."

Dinner, gift, and entertainment: I sighed and congratulated myself for doing a good job with the evening. I'd been concocting birthday parties for Chloé since her mother left, and every year was a challenge.

"Heads up," she said quietly. "She's on her way."

I understood and nonchalantly nodded.

And there she was, the curly-haired trumpet player, saying, "Andy, I was so surprised to see you here. And Chloé, I'm Shannon. We met after the ballet and at your apartment party too."

Chloé smiled warmly. "I remember. Nice to see you again. It's my birthday celebration. Would you like to have a drink with us?"

I could have thwacked Chloé for the invitation. It was already after 11:00 and I had to work the next day. Besides, I couldn't think of anything to say to the pretty musician.

"I'd love to, but I'm here with my sister, visiting from..."

Chloé cut her off with, "Bring over two chairs. We'll squeeze in."

Ten minutes later, we were a group of four. I ordered another seltzer. I'd be tired the next morning, but at least I'd have a clear head. Shannon asked for the same, and her sister ordered a decaf coffee. Chloé asked for a second Kuhlua on the rocks.

The sister had the same curly brown hair as Shannon, but cut short. "I'm three years younger than my talented sister," she said.

"True," Shannon quipped, "Sherri doesn't have any talent at all."

I tried to shift into chit-chat mode with a standard question: "What do you do, Sherri?"

Shannon answered for her, "She's the assistant registrar at Boston University. In other words, she's a computer whiz." She sliced her hand over her head and added, "Very very intelligent."

"Like Chloé," I said, pointing to my left. "Physical therapist and researcher."

Shannon touched my arm. "We've talked, Andy, but I don't know what you do."

This time, Chloé answered for me. "He's the best fragrance salesperson at Bergdorf Goodman."

I felt my face get hot. "I've been there for a long time," I said.

"I love that store," Shannon said.

"I'm in town for two more days," Sherri said. "We'll come by, if I can tear Shannon away from her work.

Rehearsals during the day, performances at night, it's never-ending."

"Did you skip a performance tonight because of Sherri's visit?" Chloé asked.

"No. I got lucky. Tonight's ballet was *A Simple Symphony*. It's a string orchestra piece by Benjamin Britten. No trumpets! So I got the night off to entertain my little sis."

I jumped in, "You should get lucky again," and immediately regretted saying it. It sounded like I was propositioning her. I couldn't erase the words from the air, so I went on, "We still need to find a time for Ned's payoff after losing the bet at Chloé's apartment party."

"I was there when he promised lunch for everyone, if you need a witness," Chloé said.

"I was impressed that night that you remembered I was a trumpet player."

I shrugged with a grin. "I always wanted to be a saxophone player. So I guess I felt a kindred spirit."

"I didn't know that, Daddy," Chloé said, surprised.

"Did you have lessons?" Sherri asked.

I felt embarrassed talking about myself, but I answered, "My mother's a big believer in all the arts. She made me take piano lessons for two years when I was a kid, but it was clear that I had no gift for playing." I mimed doing an arpeggio on a piano, then put my hands over my ears because of the terrible sound.

"Wow," Shannon exclaimed.

I thought she liked my Marcel Marceau imitation, but I was wrong. Her eyes were dancing when she said, "Your jacket has very snazzy lining."

It wasn't my clever personality that got her attention, but my new tan sport coat that gaped open when I'd covered my ears.

I held out one side of the jacket, and she cried, "Yes, I love the parrots!"

Chloé and Sherri laughed agreement. I had to admit, I liked the wild jungle scene too. Joey Belton, the salesperson in the Men's Store, had had good instincts about the size 38R sport coat.

Shannon took a drink of seltzer and looked at me seriously, "You know, Andy, I have a friend who plays the sax. He used to be in the NYCB orchestra, a nice guy. I'll ask him to give you a few free lessons to see if you like the instrument."

I shook my head No, but Chloé answered before I could speak. "That's a great idea, Daddy. You should do it."

The three women looked at me expectantly. I'd daydreamed about volunteering as a D.J. someday, maybe after I retired, something to make me feel like a I was part of the music world. But playing? "I'm too old to start something new," I said.

"Too old!" Shannon exclaimed. "No."

Sherri pushed in with, "Shannon's two sons are in their late 20's…"

"Like me," Chloé inserted.

273

"…And you wouldn't call my sister too old, would you?" Sherri pushed.

I was sure that my face was beet red, like I'd fallen into a vat of hot water. "Of course not," I said to Shannon. "You're young and energetic and…"

"Just like you are, Daddy."

"I'll tell you what," Shannon pressed on. "Barry is playing at Birdland Jazz for a month with the Louis Armstrong Eternity Band. They have a 5:30 show almost every day. You can hear him play, I'll introduce you, and you can schedule a meeting with him."

"Oh Daddy, yes," Chloé pressed. "It sounds like fun for you."

There was that idiotic word "fun." Less than two hours before, I had wished for more fun. Did that obligate me to agree to Shannon's crazy offer? Curses on birthday candle wishes.

"I haven't been to Birdland in a very long time," I said, avoiding a concrete answer.

Sherri turned toward Shannon and said, "I think that qualifies as a Yes, big sis. I've never been there; it'll be something new for me."

At least, I'd have a chaperone, I thought.

Shannon looked at me and said, "I think it's better if we go by ourselves."

Sherri and Chloé had the same reaction, pulling their chins back in surprise at her statement.

Shannon asked me, "Can you be at 44th and 8th around 5:30 tomorrow? We won't be able to stay long. I

274

have to be at Koch Theater by 7:00 to play for the evening's show. But we'll have enough time to talk and listen and enjoy ourselves."

Whether I wanted to go or not, I had been railroaded by three woman into a date with a trumpet player. Yes, it sounded like a date, not an appointment or meeting. It was a date with a curly-haired female who had announced she wanted to be alone with me.

Was it because of the McQueen black jeans? Did they make me look sexy? Ready for fun? In the loop? A la mode? Modern and forward thinking? If that was it, the jeans were lying. I didn't feel sexy at all, and certainly I wasn't ready for a date.

But the idea of a trying out a saxophone, that idea was like a magnet.

"Would I need to buy a sax to have a lesson?" I asked.

Sherri answered for her sister, "Shannon's apartment is decorated with instruments. She has recorders, flutes, and trombones mounted on the walls as if she were displaying trophy tigers and bears."

Shannon pointed at her sister, "You be quiet." Then to me, she said, "Are you going to want an alto or tenor sax?"

"Which would you suggest?"

She shrugged. "I have a couple of both, and a baritone and bass too." She ducked her head like she was embarrassed and added, "But I don't have a soprano sax."

"You're saying I could borrow one?" I was amazed. "I'd be careful with it and get it back to you right after the lesson. That is," I looked down at my hands clinched in my lap, "that is, if your friend is interested in meeting with me. I'm an absolute novice."

I had gotten ahead of myself; it sounded like I had agreed go with Shannon to meet Barry at Birdland. Chloé was nodding at me, as if she was silently saying, "Try it. You can always back out later. Go ahead."

I took a deep breath and nodded. "Okay. Let's meet tomorrow at 5:30. I look forward to seeing you."

Fifteen minutes later, on the sidewalk outside Carolines, I held my doggy bag of chicken parm and spaghetti, and watched Shannon and Sherri wave goodbye.

My daughter looked at me with a grin as if she expected me to say something, so I did: "Let's take a taxi. It's too late to go on the bus."

I didn't wait for her answer and started looking up and down Broadway. Three cabs passed us, none of them available.

"What will you wear on your date tomorrow?" Chloé asked with a laughing lilt in her voice.

I ignored her. Another taxi came toward us, this one with its light on, and I raised my hand to hail it.

She was still chuckling to herself when I told the driver, "Two stops: first at Amsterdam and 69th; second at West End Avenue and 98th." The cabbie was driving by the time Chloé slammed the door shut.

I pressed my lips together, feeling mad, because I was reviewing my closet to see what clothes might impress Shannon at Birdland the next day. I gave up and gave into Chloé's question. "Nothing too dressy," I answered.

That set Chloé off on a guffaw so loud the driver looked at us in the rearview mirror.

When she calmed down, she agreed, "Nothing too dressy. But you'll be coming from work; you'll have on a tie and jacket."

She was right. An early evening date, to hear jazz and to meet a potential music teacher, what was the dress code for a rendezvous like that?

"Too bad you can't wear what you have on now. But she'd notice if you showed up in the same clothes. She'd probably think you stayed out all night without her." She cracked up filling the cab with a belly laugh.

"Me going to hear music is so funny?" I pouted.

She kept laughing, "Oh Daddy, yes, very funny."

I crossed my arms across my chest.

She put her hand on my arm, "Also, it's very endearing. You deserve a date. I love Shannon's big curly hair. She seems genuinely nice. I bet you have a good time. And you're going to learn to play the sax!"

I did not uncross my arms or smile, but after a beat, I said, "I have another new Armani t-shirt like this one, but in aqua marine. I'll get the tailor at Bergdorf to wash and dry the jeans before tomorrow evening."

This sent Chloé into another spasm of laughter.

277

§§

The hammering wouldn't stop. Was someone building a doghouse for Blue? No. It must be someone putting in new windows on the 5th Avenue side of the store.

"Daddy."

Was Chloé building something?

"Daddy, where are you? Daddy!"

Oh, I couldn't move my hand. It was stuck under my cheek tingling with pins and needles. I opened my eyes.

It was my bathroom. I was on the floor.

Someone was knocking on the apartment door. I closed my eyes again.

"Oh Daddy," Chloé repeated from close range, and suddenly I saw her crouched beside me.

"He's here, Nana. Call 911."

I took a deep breath and pushed myself up on an elbow. "Hi Honey. What are you doing here?"

Nana rushed in with a phone to her ear. "I knew I'd outlast him," she was saying. "But I thought since he'd lost all the weight, he'd…"

I sat up and assessed the situation. I was wearing shorts and a tee-shirt, no socks. My cell phone was next to me. "How'd you get in my apartment?" I asked.

Nana changed gears and spoke in her disdainful tone: "Your daughter didn't want to be by herself when she found you dead, so she called me. I have a duplicate set of

278

your keys, if you remember." She put her hands on her hips and spoke to Chloé while she pointed at me in disgust, "I left my canvas for that. Clearly, he's not dying." Pissed off, she clapped shut her phone before the emergency call went through.

I had to put my hand on the bowl of the toilet to lift myself off the floor. "No, I'm not dying. And if I were, I'd have pushed the gizmo on my ankle." There it was, just above my foot, the ankle bracelet with the emergency button waiting for me to fall victim to my rotten heart. "I've worn it almost a week."

Nana left the bathroom but kept talking. "Look at these clothes dropped on the floor, from the door to the bedroom. You had a drunken liaison, didn't you, Andy? And you didn't mind scaring us in the process."

"What's she talking about, Chloé?" I asked my daughter.

She handed me my robe from the hook on the bathroom door. "When you didn't answer your phone, I was so worried, Daddy. Why didn't you answer your phone?"

I tied the belt of the navy blue Hanro robe, picked up my phone from the tile floor, looked at it, and put it in my pocket, like a boy hiding a stolen candy bar.

Chloé rolled her eyes. That was when it dawned on me, she wasn't smiling. "Come into the living room and sit down," she said.

Nana continued blaring, "Here's more proof. A saxophone. She left it, didn't she? That saxophone woman,

279

the one from the ballet orchestra, right? And what? After you two bedded down, you threw up and passed out in the bathroom, and she went on her merry way?"

I sat on the couch and faced Nana's glare as she kept talking: "You were thinking with your prick, while poor Chloé here was scared to death about her father. Shame on you, Andy."

The apartment door opened, and Chloé cried, "Oh Cary, I should have called to let you know. He's here. He's fine."

"A waste of our time is what he is," Nana growled.

"Andy," Cary said, coming toward me. "Good to see you looking well." He sat beside me on the couch. "What happened?"

That was a logical question, the first one I'd heard since my home had been invaded. "Good to see you too, Cary," I answered. "I had a heck of a night." I steered my glance toward my mother, "A night *alone*!" Chloé sat on the other side of me.

"Then what's the meaning of *this*?" she demanded, picking my black jeans off the floor with her thumb and forefinger.

Chloé took my hand in hers. "And I called you so many times," she said earnestly.

"Why did you call?" I asked.

"You didn't show up at your appointment with Brad. You didn't show up and didn't answer his calls, so he phoned me to find out if something had happened. Oh god, I was so scared."

280

I shook my head as if I had water in my ears. "I didn't show up? What time is it?"

Cary looked at his watch. "It's 10:24."

I leapt up and screeched. "10:24? I have to get to work. Everybody out so I can get to work. I'm going to be late!"

"You're not going anywhere," Nana commanded. "Not until you tell me what happened last night."

I bumbled my way over Chloé's legs to move past the coffee table. But Cary's calm voice stopped me, "Why don't you call Ryker and tell him you need a sick day? Or a ½ day? Then we can all have a cup of coffee, some breakfast together, and you can re-start your day. How's that?"

The man had an unflappable benevolence that seemed to embrace the room. It was probably the characteristic that had enabled him to stay with my mother all these years.

"Call Ryker," he repeated, "and I'll make coffee." He maneuvered me back onto the couch before he made his way to the kitchen.

I pulled my phone out of the robe's pocket and dialed Bergdorf's. When I reached Ryker, I said, "I'm having a disorganized morning."

He chuckled on his end of the conversation. "Good disorganized or bad?" he asked.

"I'll tell you when I get there. I'll be late."

He snorted, "Stay away as long as you can. I'm taking your customers."

It was the first smile of my morning. "Don't you dare," I threatened and hung up.

"And you have to call Brad to let him know you're okay," Chloé said.

"Brad?" I asked.

She looked at me like I had had a stroke. "Bradley Matthews. You know, you've seen him every week since your heart attack."

I smiled again and nodded. She was talking about Ponytail. I didn't have his number on my contact list, but I searched Mount Sinai and finally got connected to his voice mail. "Hello. It's Andy Brown. Sorry I missed our appointment. I'll be there next week as usual."

Nana plopped down in a chair with a pile of my clothes on the floor next to her. "That wasn't much of an explanation for your personal care-taker," she sniped.

I ignored her and focused on Cary carrying in a tray with four coffee cups. The aroma made me gag. I rubbed the back of my neck and explained, "Yesterday afternoon, I met Shannon Shriver at Birdland, I borrowed a saxophone from a guy there, and at 7:30, I was on my way home when the worst stomach spasms of my life descended on me. And I do mean *descended*." My stomach lurched with the memory.

Nana and Cary stirred sugar in their coffee. Mine sat on the coffee table untouched. Chloé sipped her black coffee and repeated, "Spasms?"

"We had hors-d'oeuvres during the music at Birdland, chicken kabobs with an Indian sauce. It must

282

have been from that. I should call Shannon to see if she was sick too."

I picked up my phone, but Nana spat out an order: "No! Finish your story first."

I rubbed my temple with my right hand and my stomach with my left hand. "I took a bus instead of walking home. Half-way here, I thought I was going to explode. My stomach was gurgling, my intestines were squeezing, and, well, all I can say is, by the time I ran into the building and into the elevator, I was already unbuttoning my pants. Inside I ripped off my clothes and barely got to the bathroom in time. Oh my god, what a disaster." I started sweating as I remembered.

"Some kind of food poisoning," Chloé said, always the diagnostician.

"I'm lucky it didn't start at Birdland in front of Shannon. All night, I had the trots. I threw up twice in between the diarrhea and cramps. I'd think it was over, and a half hour later, I'd run to the royal throne again. At 3:00 in the morning, I just stayed in the bathroom, waiting for the next onslaught of crap."

"It sounds bad," Cary commiserated.

"I've never been sick like that," I said. "I must have fallen asleep on the floor in the bathroom."

Nana's nose was in the air as if she were sniffing for disgusting odors.

Chloé put her hand on my arm and said, "Did you sleep through your phone ringing? I called so many times."

I patted her hand. My daughter had been worried. I was sorry she had gone through that, but it felt good that she was concerned about me.

"I wasn't avoiding you," I explained. "Between the nasty intestinal eruptions, I entertained myself by scrolling through Facebook. I turned off the sound so I didn't have to listen to the annoying ads."

She rested her head on my shoulder, letting her red glasses shift to the side. "I'm glad you're okay, Daddy."

"Me too, honey," I told her.

Cary clapped his hands. "I'm sure your stomach is still sensitive. Don't drink that coffee, Andy. I'll make you something to calm your digestive system." And he was off to the kitchen again.

Nana shook her head. "That man. He's always managing things."

She was right. He even managed her.

"So tell us about this Shannon person," Nana demanded.

I settled back on the couch and crossed my legs.

"Oh, I see a smile," Chloé cooed. "That means he had a good time."

I couldn't keep a straight face. "Yes, the music was good."

Chloé pinched my bicep. "It wasn't the music."

"No, really, Ostwald's band played great tunes from the 1920's. Six musicians, swing and soul for over an hour. Sherry's friend Barry Friedman was terrific on saxophone. We scheduled a lesson for this Sunday afternoon. He loaned me a sax just so I could, I don't know, so I could get the feel of it "

Cary entered with a tray and set it on the coffee table. "Dry toast, a banana, and seltzer for you, Andy. Everything else is for us," he said with a grin, while he bit off the corner of a strawberry Pop Tart. Nana took a boiled egg and put a slice of ham on her buttered toast. Chloé put butter on two Eggos and poured maple syrup over them.

"Bravo for diving into music, Andy," he said. "I always thought you had a hidden talent there."

Cary had never said a negative word to me, but also he'd never pushed me in one direction or another. I wished he had mentioned 37 years ago that he thought I had a hidden talent.

"But I want to hear about this *woman*," my mother said in a sarcastic voice, as if she meant to say *slut*.

"Yes, tell us everything," Chloé tittered.

I swallowed a bite of toast and put my arm around Chloé's shoulders. "She has children of her own, you know."

"I'm 27 years old, Daddy. I don't need another mother. Tell me what you thought about Shannon."

I nodded like a teenager. "Yes, well, I liked her. She's funny. She loves music."

"She's pretty," Chloé prompted.

"Yes, she's pretty. And she seems sort of interested in me." I felt my face get hot.

It was Cary who asked the big question, "Did you kiss her?"

I moaned, "No. We didn't kiss. It was still daylight when we came out of Birdland."

"You shook her hand?" Nana asked, cringing.

"No, I didn't shake her hand. But we agreed to meet Friday. Just to get a bite to eat together before she goes to work." My stomach heaved, and I set the toast down. "If I can keep food down by then," I added.

"It was the sauce," Nana declared. "Indian sauces go bad very quickly." She set her plate down. "That's why they call it Delhi Belly."

"Nana," Chloé chided mildly, "racist phrases don't help."

"Of course they do. You knew exactly what I meant."

"Thank you for not repeating it a second time," Chloé chuckled.

Nana slapped her hands on her knees and turned to me. "Now that I know you're alive, I'm going back to my painting." She gave me a serious look. "Don't scare us again."

Cary stood up with my mother. "I'll just clear these things away and go too."

"No, no," I said. "Leave it. I'll do it later."

As Chloé followed them to the door, I kept my arm around her shoulders. "I appreciate you rushing over here, Chloé," I said.

"I'm glad it was a false alarm, Daddy." She hugged me and left with the others.

Nana walked to the elevator holding Cary's arm, and over her shoulder, she informed me, "You need a shower, Andy."

I closed the door behind them and let myself go limp. Concerned visitors were okay, but it was much easier to feel crumby without having to be polite. I went back to the couch and picked up the phone.

When Ryker answered my call, I said smiling, "I've got to take a sick day. You'll never believe why." It was the same story I'd told my family, except with the added details about one hour of timidly touching a beautiful woman in a dimly lit club.

§§

Ponytail looked at me with his light brown eyes. "Mr. Brown, it's good to see you. I was relieved to get your message last week."

"Yes, about that," I said. "I'm sorry for not showing up for our appointment. I had an intestinal flu bug and overslept."

Ponytail had on a bright blue tie with thin white diagonal stripes. Silk, I was sure. Probably Briani. Or Charvet. He always wore good ties. In fact, he was a good looking man. Maybe I'd grow a ponytail of my own. My hair was still thick, or at least thick enough to have another go at looking like a hippie. My Bergdorf clients would love teasing me about it, and I'd love the attention.

"You've recovered?" he asked.

I nodded. "Yes, thank you. Just a 24 hour thing. Ah…, you called my daughter?"

Ponytail cleared his throat and folded his hands on his desk behind his name plate announcing him as Bradley Matthews, APRN, CVRN, MSN, DNP. He said, "You have responded well to the stents, the reduced medications, and the weight loss. But you had never missed an appointment. Your daughter and mother are listed as your emergency contacts, so I called to make sure you were okay."

I smiled. "You mean you wondered if I was dead on the bathroom floor?"

He smirked agreement.

"That's what Chloé thought. The bathroom, yes, dead, no," I laughed. Then I lifted my right leg and rolled down my sock. "And my emergency gizmo was in reach if I had needed."

"I have to say, having it on your ankle is an excellent idea. You wear it all the time, right?"

"All the time," I answered.

"Good. Let's get today's exam started," he said.

We went through the entire thing: blood pressure reading, blood sample, thumping the chest front and back, deep breaths, and listening to my heart from every direction possible. I blew into a lung-capacity device. Then with me on the table at the side of his office, he did a sonogram reading of my chest and neck; we ended with the scales.

"Do you want to say it out loud?" Ponytail asked, looking at the digital readout of my weight. "Or shall I?"

I tried to hide my grin. "You," I answered.

"Mr. Brown, you weigh 188 pounds. Congratulations."

Okay, I didn't look great. I was still 5'9", compared to the over 6 feet of someone like Ponytail, and I had baggy skin and wrinkles around my eyes. But I had never before looked slim, not in my entire life. I didn't need a mirror to know I was a good-looking fellow, considering who I was.

"It wasn't so hard to lose weight," I said. "I mean, I didn't diet or anything."

"I know. You walked and told secrets. Maybe your daughter will write an article about you."

"Funny you should say that. She's started a research project about heart attack patients and their weight changes." I shrugged and added, "But she won't use me in it because I'm family."

Ponytail typed something on his tablet and pushed it aside. "I'll get your blood test results in a couple of days, but unless there is something unexpected there, we'll assume you are in good health."

I took a deep breath, feeling like I could tame a wild lion.

"It's been six months since your heart attack."

It seemed like it had been a couple of weeks, I thought. Then again, it seemed like the heart attack had happened during another lifetime.

"So our weekly meetings are over," Ponytail said. "I want you to come back in six months for a thorough exam, or of course, if you have any symptoms or distress, call and I'll see you immediately. But I expect you will stay heart-healthy for a very long time."

"You mean I've graduated?"

Ponytail smiled. "You've graduated."

"So, we're finished?" I asked, not quite sure of the protocol for leaving this forced relationship.

He kept smiling, "Yes, we're finished. You can go."

I stood up, "Okay then."

He stood up as well. "There's one other thing," he said and paused.

I waited.

"Since you will no longer be my patient, I was wondering," he seemed to be looking for words, "I was wondering if it would be alright with you…, ah, I mean, would you mind if…"

If he shared my story in a medical journal? If I would give him a discount at Bergdorf Goodman? What?

"…if I called your daughter?"

I didn't understand. He had already called Chloé. He'd called her a few times.

"…called her to go out with me, I mean." His expression was serious, like he was about to speak in front of a jury.

"You want to take Chloé on a date?" I asked, laughing. There could be worse things than having a tall guy with good taste in clothes go out with Chloé. "Well, it's okay with me, but I'm not in charge of what she'll say or do." I wouldn't warn her about the call, but I'd be interested how she reacted to a call from Ponytail.

I stuck my hand out, and across the desk, we shook. I glanced at his name plate and said, "Thank you, Mr. Matthews, for your help during these six months."

"My pleasure," he answered.

"You want to ask my daughter out on a date." I laughed again and turned to leave. "That's a good one."

The End

M.D. Poole

Author of *Bergdorf Goodman, The Dentist, Transatlantic, Lucky Larsen, Dogs Never Lie, Just Across the Street in New York City,* and *Verna Ware's Long Way Home*, Poole has also written four detective novels, *Cowtown Crime, Cowtown Corpse, Cowtown Cop*, and *Cowtown Coffin*, featuring Detective Frank "Pink" Bettman.

Poole's poetry is available under the title *Children of Eve*. She has authored the short story collection *Sundog Stories*, as well as *Hogan the Horse BedTime Tales* for children. Six of Poole's plays have been produced off-Broadway and in regional theater. Her writing has appeared in 25 books and journals. Her blog is found at www.mdpoole.wordpress.com

Poole has over ten years' experience writing scripts for television and radio advertising, as well as working with Barnes & Noble Bookstores, New York City Opera at Lincoln Center (on stage and off), and Van Cleef & Arpels. Poole has owned and managed three businesses, Private Drawers, Barkley Dogs, and Word Doctor.

Dr. Poole earned her PhD in English Language and Literature from TCU. She served as the director of the Deep South Writers Conference while teaching at Southwestern Louisiana University prior to taking a position at the State University of New York FIT in New York City. She lives in France. Her interests include ballet, travel, quilting, and dogs.

Made in United States
North Haven, CT
11 January 2023

30887297R00163